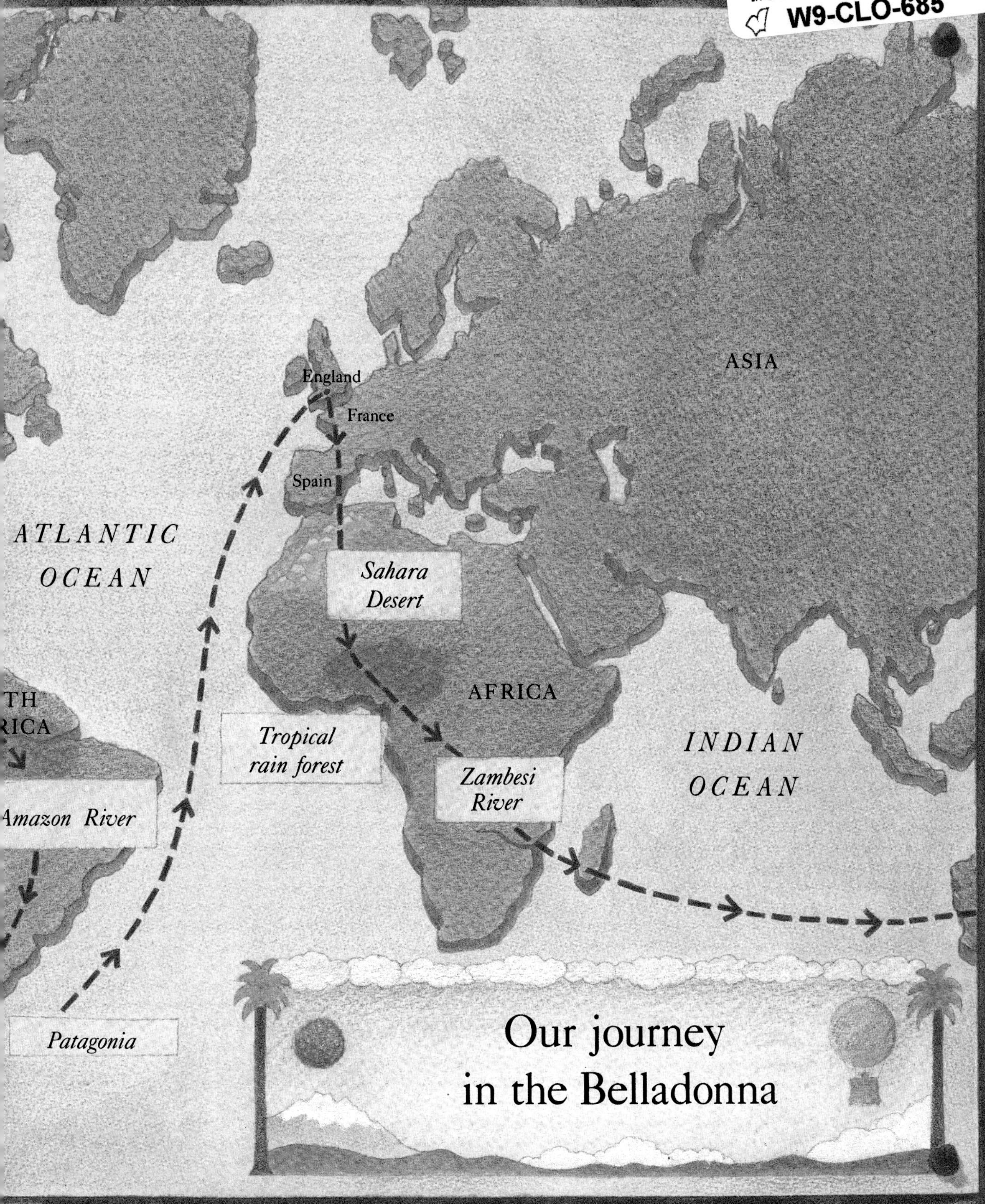

ASIA

ATLANTIC
OCEAN

England

France

Spain

Sahara
Desert

AFRICA

INDIAN
OCEAN

TH
RICA

Tropical
rain forest

Zambesi
River

Amazon River

Patagonia

Our journey
in the Belladonna

The Fantastic Flying Journey

The Fantastic Flying Journey

by GERALD DURRELL

illustrated by Graham Percy

SIMON AND SCHUSTER BOOKS FOR YOUNG READERS
Published by Simon & Schuster Inc., New York

SIMON AND SCHUSTER
BOOKS FOR YOUNG READERS
Simon & Schuster Building
Rockefeller Center
1230 Avenue of the Americas
New York, New York 10020

Copyright © 1987 by Gerald Durrell
Artwork copyright © 1987 by Conran Octopus Limited

Originally published in Great Britain by Conran Octopus Limited
SIMON AND SCHUSTER BOOKS FOR YOUNG READERS
is a trademark of Simon & Schuster Inc.
Title Calligraphy by Golda Laurens
Manufactured in the United States of America
10   9   8   7   6   5   4   3   2   1
Library of Congress Cataloging–in–Publication Data
Durrell, Gerald Malcolm, 1925–
The fantastic flying journey.
SUMMARY: Great–Uncle Lancelot, redoubtable
explorer and enthusiastic naturalist, takes his
niece and twin nephews on an extraordinary journey
around the world, introducing them to a wide variety of animals.
[1. Animals—Fiction.   2. Voyages around the
world—Fiction]   I. Percy, Graham, ill.   II. Title.
PZ7.D9343Fan   1988   [Fic]   87-20750
ISBN 0-671-64982-5

for
SAMANTHA
and the
twins,
GENEVIEVE AND OLIVIA,
with love
from
GERRY PA

Contents

The Fantastic Flying Journey

CHAPTER ONE

AN UNEXPECTED VISITOR

The whole thing started out of the blue. The Dollybutt children had been collecting mushrooms in the woods and fields around their cottage. Emma, who at fifteen was the eldest, had blue eyes and blonde hair. Her brothers, Conrad and Ivan, were identical twins. They were twelve years old, each with hair the color of chestnuts and snub noses so covered with freckles that they looked like two thrushes' eggs.

They had succeeded in gathering a big basketful of creamy-colored mushrooms and were making their way back to the cottage when, suddenly, it seemed as if the sun had gone behind a cloud. An enormous shadow fell across the cottage garden. The children were amazed to hear a loud, roaring voice coming from high above them.

"Ahoy! Ahoy! You down there, you children," the voice shouted.

Emma and the twins looked up, open-mouthed, and saw the most wonderful and amazing sight.

Up above them was a huge, multicolored balloon, iridescent as a soap bubble. Slung beneath it was an extraordinary structure made out of bamboo. It looked like a gigantic laundry basket, but it had windows, shutters and a front door. On the very top was a sort of veranda with three large telescopes on it, and peeping over the side was a huge, white beard and walrus moustache.

"You down there," continued the roaring voice, which sounded as though its owner had spent his life gargling with gravel. "Are you the Dollybutt children?"

"Yes, we are," replied Emma, "but who on earth are you?"

"I'm your Great-Uncle Lancelot, of course. Hasn't your mother told you all about me?"

The children shook their heads. The moustache twitched impatiently.

"Well, give me a hand here and I'll be down in a jiffy."

Lancelot threw two long ropes of fine silk and asked the children to tie each one to a tree. There was a gentle hiss, like a basketful of cobras singing to themselves, as Lancelot let the air out of the balloon. The great basket settled, creaking and groaning, onto the lawn and, I regret to say, on Mrs. Dollybutt's favorite rose bed as well. The door opened and Great-Uncle Lancelot appeared.

He swept off his hat and, to Emma's great embarrassment, seized her hand and kissed it. His moustache and beard were so bristly that she felt as if she had put her hand into a haystack.

"You must be Emma," he remarked, standing back to look at her. "And you must be Ivan and Conrad, although goodness only knows which of you is which."

He shook hands vigorously with them both as they solemnly told him their names.

"Splendid, splendid to meet you at last," he continued, as the children stared at him open-mouthed. "Don't look so surprised to see me. Shake a leg and take me inside to see your mother."

The children led the way into the cottage. When they entered the kitchen, poor Mrs. Dollybutt was so startled by Lancelot's loud roar of greeting that she dropped the plate of biscuits she was holding all over the floor. Lancelot clasped her tight in his arms and planted a smacking kiss on each of her rosy cheeks.

"Sally, my girl, it's good to see you again," he said, gazing at her fondly. "I've been away for far too long."

"It's . . . er . . . lovely to see you, Lancelot," Mrs. Dollybutt replied nervously. "Very nice . . . um . . . How did you get here?"

"In my balloon," said Lancelot. "It's the only way to travel. I've tried everything—camel caravans, yak trains, ships, airplanes, the lot, but without a doubt, balloons are the best and the most peaceful way to travel."

"Very nice, I'm sure," responded Mrs. Dollybutt, uncertainly, "but are they really safe?"

"Of course they are," came the answer as Lancelot sat down on a chair that creaked protestingly at his weight. "Safe as houses. Why, are you worried about the children coming with me?"

"What?" shrieked Mrs. Dollybutt. "What are you talking about?"

"Didn't you get my telegram?" asked Lancelot, tugging at his huge moustache in annoyance. Mrs. Dollybutt shook her head.

"We're going to search for Perceval," explained Lancelot. "He went off to study gorillas in Africa and hasn't returned."

"Who is Perceval?" asked Conrad.

"He is my brother, your other great-uncle," replied Lancelot. "He's been gone for two years, and I'm very worried. I'm going to search for him, and I need your sharp eyes and ears to help me. Goodness knows where he's got to. We may have to go right around the world before we find him."

"But in a *balloon?*" wailed Mrs. Dollybutt.

"Of course!" roared Lancelot. "The children will be perfectly safe. This will be the greatest adventure of their lives and I won't

take no for an answer."

"What about school?" gasped Mrs. Dollybutt.

"I'll fix that," said Lancelot firmly. "I'll phone the headmaster. A trip in Belladonna will be far more interesting."

"Oh dear!" wailed Mrs. Dollybutt. "They'll be expelled."

"No they won't," retorted Lancelot, ferociously. "If he tries anything like that, I'll go down to the school personally and tear him in half, possibly into quarters."

The children chuckled at this novel way of dealing with their stern and dignified headmaster.

"And what about me?" asked Mrs. Dollybutt, lamely, knowing that once Lancelot's mind was made up, there was no changing it.

"You're going on a holiday to London, my girl," said Lancelot. "My wife, Conchita, is going to show you a good old time."

"But I can't possibly afford it," gasped Mrs. Dollybutt.

"Maybe not, but I can," said Lancelot. "Thanks to a small but well-stocked gold mine I discovered in Peru, I've got a fair bit of money. Now, no more arguments. Come outside, children, and I'll show you Belladonna."

A closer look at Belladonna revealed that she was shaped like a tower with a circular staircase running up the middle. The whole thing was divided into several floors, on the lowest of which were the living room, storerooms, kitchen and pantry.

"She's the finest balloon of her kind," began Lancelot. "I built her myself, of course. The outside is made of several different sorts of bamboo, which is light and flexible. The inside is lined with musk-ox wool, for insulation. Beneath your feet here is a large tank containing electric eels. They supply the electricity for the fridge and the electric lights. Of course, it takes a little time to teach them to give the right current to the right buttons, but it does work."

The children followed him up the staircase. To their astonishment, the whole of the first floor was a small garden with rows and rows of vegetables and miniature fruit trees. Vines hung from the ceiling.

"It's wonderful," said Emma. "It's a flying farm."

"Look at that delicious fruit," said Conrad, licking his lips.

"Help yourself," said Lancelot, smiling, as the children plucked plump succulent apples, red as the setting sun.

In among the apple trees were three large cages of spiders.

"They spin the silk for the balloon and all the rope ladders and things," explained Lancelot. "I have to keep them on board to do repairs. I change them from time to time. Fortunately, both the eels and spiders come from the same part of South America. Most convenient. Now, up we go."

On their way to the flight deck on the very top of Belladonna, they passed four neat little bedrooms. "Sleeping quarters," boomed Lancelot.

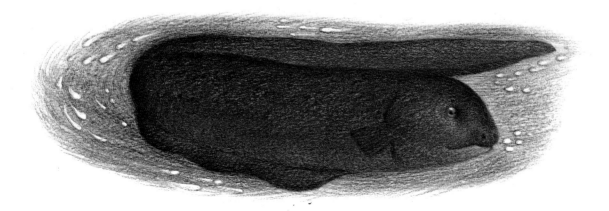

The flight deck, as Lancelot called it, was a small cabin on the veranda. It was full of charts, maps and instruments.

"I have a small diesel engine which I designed myself," said Lancelot proudly. "It runs entirely off the sap of a South American tree called *Copaifera*. Splendid stuff. It heats the hot air for the balloon and also drives a small propellor, so that I can steer. Solar panels heat the water for cooking and washing."

"It's great," said Ivan. "It's a real floating home."

"Quite," said Lancelot. "Well, you've seen everything now. Come downstairs and we'll start making plans for our journey."

When they were all comfortably seated in the living room, Lancelot cleared his throat. "Now, listen carefully," he said. "We may have to travel thousands of miles to find Perceval. We will meet many dangers on our journey, so you must be properly prepared. But this is not just a rescue mission, you know."

"What do you mean?" interrupted Conrad, rather rudely.

Lancelot gave him a fierce look, then smiled.

"The world is full of wonderful questions to be answered."

"Like how balloons can fly?" asked Ivan, laughing.

"Exactly," nodded Lancelot, "and what makes an acorn the size of the end of your thumb grow into a tree over sixty feet tall that is home for fifty creatures? Where do birds fly to in winter? How do fish swim? There are millions of questions and this trip will show you the answers to some of them. So you must keep your noses tilted for smells, your tongues ready for tastes, your fingers poised to touch, and your ears and eyes open to explore and enjoy."

"Wow!" said Conrad. "You make it sound terrific."

"It will be," said Lancelot. "And now I'm going to make it even more terrific."

He went over to the cupboard and took out a green bottle. He put it on the table.

"This is Perceval's," he explained. "My brother is a great scientist who has discovered many things. This is his most special and important invention."

He opened the bottle, poured a small amount of gray powder into a spoon and sprinkled it over Emma. As she watched, the powder quickly disappeared into her skin. She rubbed the back of her hand in amazement, but the curious substance had completely vanished. Lancelot then sprinkled the twins in the same way.

Suddenly they all heard a ringing in their ears, like a chorus of tiny bells. This grew very loud for a moment, then died away.

"Now," ordered Lancelot, "come outside with me."

On the telephone wires sat a long line of swallows, twittering to each other as they prepared for their winter migration.

"What are they saying?" Lancelot asked Emma.

"Why," said Emma, "they're giving one another hints about the journey they're going to make . . ."

She stopped short and stared at Lancelot in amazement.

"But I can understand them!" she cried delightedly. "I know what they're saying."

"Quite," said Lancelot. "It's almost like magic. From now on you will be able to understand and talk to every animal you meet. You can learn a lot more from animals if you can ask them questions."

The children were overwhelmed with delight at their new accomplishment. The twins ran off to talk to a hedgehog they knew, while Emma listened entranced to the swallows.

"One of those birds could guide us much better than a map," said Lancelot. "We're going first to the Sahara Desert, which is in Africa, and that's where swallows migrate for the winter."

"These ones are just about to fly off," said Emma, "but I expect there are still some left in the barn."

There was only one, however, a rather disgruntled-looking specimen, sitting on the edge of his nest.

"Ahoy there, Swallow," called Lancelot. "Would you like a lift to Africa on our balloon in return for a little navigation?"

"What would I eat?" demanded Swallow. "I can't live on air."

"Mealworms," said Lancelot, enticingly. "I've got a big box."

"I'll give it some thought," said Swallow, "but it sounds like a lot of bother to me. When are you leaving?"

"Tomorrow morning," said Lancelot. "Early."

"Come and see me then," said Swallow. "I'll consider your offer and let you know."

The next morning, having seen Mrs. Dollybutt safely off on her trip to London, they went to the barn. It was empty. Swallow had already flown up to the flight deck and was waiting for them to board Belladonna. Everything was ready for the fabulous flying journey. The children had never been so excited in their lives.

CHAPTER TWO

A FLYING
START

The silken ropes were pulled in and coiled neatly. Like a huge
soap bubble, Belladonna rose majestically into the air and
swooped to the south, gaining height all the time. Hanging over
the railings, the children watched the multicolored countryside
slide away below them. The sounds of cocks crowing, cars
honking and even people talking floated up through the still,
clear air.

As they climbed higher, the towns and villages grew smaller
and smaller. Soon, the cows and sheep looked like ants. With the
aid of the telescopes, of course, the children could see things
long before they reached them and this added to the fun.

One of the things that astonished the children most was the
silence. Belladonna floated quietly through the sky like a
dandelion puff, giving only the occasional faint hiss when hot air
was pumped into her.

Lancelot spent most of the morning on the flight deck plotting their course with the aid of Swallow. Both were in a difficult mood and the children could hear them arguing about which route to take. Their conversation echoed around the balloon.

"Perceval was last heard of studying gorillas in the African rain forest. The shortest route there is to the right of the Atlas Mountains," bellowed Lancelot in his most stubborn tone.

"And what do you know about atmospheric air currents?" retorted Swallow acidly. "That would add over sixty miles to our trip. We must keep left."

Finally, Lancelot heaved a deep sigh and gave in. He couldn't argue with a bird who did the trip twice a year. He stamped out onto the veranda and did some deep-breathing exercises to calm himself down.

"I wish I hadn't suggested bringing that wretched bird," he groaned to the children. "He's nothing but a nuisance. And so bad-tempered too!"

The children were careful not to laugh.

Lancelot clamped his eye to one of the telescopes, then uttered a roar that made the children jump.

"Look at that—the English Channel, straight ahead! How's that for navigation?" he asked, triumphantly. "Didn't need any flibbertygibbet bird to show *me* how to get there!"

The children thought the Channel was so big that you could hardly miss it, but they were tactful enough not to say so.

The Channel, dotted with tiny boats, gleamed like fish scales far below. Soon Belladonna was swooping over the fair land of France, with its rolling meadows and huge forests. Made ravenously hungry by all the fresh air, the children and Lancelot went downstairs. Lancelot, cheered by the fact that his navigation had been so accurate, cooked a huge lunch. They had sausages, mashed potatoes, fried eggs and the mushrooms the children had collected only yesterday.

After lunch, they all went back to the flight deck. Peering through the telescopes, they saw a long range of mountains ahead of them, some wearing caps of snow.

"The Pyrenees!" cried Lancelot, now in a much better humor. "We'll soon be crossing into Spain."

By nightfall, they were over central Spain. The towns and

villages below gleamed like fireflies in the balmy air.

The children went to bed, exhausted by the day's excitements. While they slept, Belladonna flew on through the night over the Mediterranean under a moon as white as a magnolia blossom and a million winking stars. The air got hotter and hotter.

The children woke to the dry, sandy smell of the desert. The sun was rising over the Sahara, which stretched as far as the eye could see. They were amazed by its wonderful colors. Some of the sand dunes were fox-red, others were butter-yellow. Where they were shaded from the rising sun, they were purple and blue. Here and there were small oases with shaggy palms that looked like green wigs flung carelessly down on the sand.

After breakfast, Lancelot took Belladonna down low to look for camels, as Emma was very keen to meet one. They swooped over the sand dunes at about thirty feet and the children, glued to the telescopes, kept watch.

Suddenly, Conrad uttered a shout.

"Look, there!" he cried. "A fox, a fox with huge ears."

"It's a Fennec fox," said Lancelot. "We'll ask him about camels. He's sure to know where to find one."

Belladonna's basket creaked onto the sand. As the children opened the front door, the heat hit them with a blast. It was just like opening an oven door.

The fox was a pale creamy color with enormous ears like furry arum lilies, bright, black eyes and a nose like a shiny, black berry. As the children approached, he wagged his tail in greeting.

"Good morning," he said, in a rather high-pitched voice. "What sort of bird lays an egg as big as that?"

"It's not an egg, it's a balloon," explained Emma, trying not to laugh.

"A balloon, eh?" said Fox, not wanting to admit that he did not know what a balloon was. "Of course, of course!"

"Have you seen any camels?" asked Conrad, impatiently.

"There's one at the oasis over there," said Fox, waving a slender paw. "I could take you to him. I wouldn't advise it, though. He's a real bore."

"I'll stay here," said Lancelot. "I'm too old and fat to go running about on sand dunes. Besides, I've met camels before."

Emma and the twins followed Fox toward the oasis. They found it difficult to walk on the soft sand. The heat was terrific and the journey was made more difficult by the rising wind which blew the sand into their faces. Their mouths felt as if they were full of grit. They were very glad to reach the cool of the oasis and drank thirstily from the pool of placid blue water.

Under one of the palms, looking very bored, sat a one-humped camel. He stared disdainfully at them for a moment then leaned

forward and put his face very close to Fox's. The next moment, uttering a strange, gurgling cry, he opened his mouth and out popped what looked like a white balloon as big as a football. Fox yelped with fright and ran off.

"Ha, ha, ha," chuckled Camel as he sucked the strange balloon-like thing back into his mouth. "It never fails, my goulla, always scares the wits out of people. He, he, he."

"But what is it?" asked Emma, who thought it looked quite disgusting, just like a monstrous piece of bubble gum.

"It's the soft palate at the top of my mouth. I can inflate it with air and out it pops," said Camel with pride. He did it again while the children watched, fascinated.

"Who are you, anyway?" Camel inquired, bored with his goulla.

"We are adventurers," said Emma, taking out the expedition diary that Mrs. Dollybutt had given her.

The camel eyed it suspiciously.

"If this is an interview," said Camel, "there'll be a fee."

"No, it's just my diary," protested Emma, indignantly, "for taking notes about the animals we meet. We're really looking for our lost Great-Uncle Perceval. He may have passed this way."

"Never heard of him," said Camel, witheringly. "If he had been here, I would have known."

"What do you mean?" interrupted Ivan.

"Human beings can't live in the desert without my help. They need me to carry them around," Camel boasted. "You see, I can go without water for a long time. I store fat in my hump for food. My padlike feet don't sink into the sand. I am. . . ."

Emma stifled a yawn. Fox had been right. Camel *was* a bore!

Quite suddenly, Camel's voice stopped. "I say," he remarked, looking around. "Don't you think it's time you got back into your balloon?"

Following his gaze, the children saw that outside the shelter of the oasis, the wind was now blowing fiercely, whipping up clouds of stinging sand. Emma and the twins looked worried.

"No need to panic," said Camel. "I'm quite used to helping travelers in the desert. I'll get you back to your balloon before the sandstorm gets any worse."

"That would be wonderful," said Emma, doubtfully.

The three children climbed up onto Camel's saddle and clung on tightly while Camel, with much humphing and groaning, got to his feet.

The children covered their noses and mouths to keep out the sand, and closed their eyes.

"Would you like my spare hankie, Camel?" asked Emma.

"Cerdenly nod," he snorted, sounding as if he had a cold.

"Why are you speaking in that funny voice?" asked Conrad.

"I'b god by nostrils closed so that the sand doesn't go ub by dose," replied Camel, impatiently. "Dow, hold on tight."

The children very soon discovered that the way a camel moves is so strange that you are hard put to it to keep your balance. First it lurches one way and then another, with a sort of swirling wriggle in the middle.

"Idn't thib the bery best ride you'b eber had?" shouted Camel.

"Oh yes," the children chorused untruthfully, thinking it was the most uncomfortable form of transport they had ever experienced. By the time they got to Belladonna they were not only sore but seasick as well.

"Thank goodness!" shouted Lancelot into the swirling sand. "I was just about to come and look for you. All aboard quickly. This wind will blow us exactly where we want to go."

The children rushed on board. Belladonna seemed to leap into the air. They waved at the fast-disappearing camel, who was soon lost in the dusty clouds as they soared southward.

By the following day the desert was far behind them. The weather was getting even hotter and the children spent most of their time in swimsuits. Lancelot changed into khaki shorts and bush jacket. His huge sun hat made him look like a giant mushroom.

"Next stop, central Africa to meet some gorillas," he boomed. "Then we can get rid of that pesky swallow."

"Hush!" warned Emma. "He might hear you."

"That'll be really exciting," said Ivan.

"Aren't gorillas dangerous?" asked Conrad.

"Not at all," Lancelot assured him. "Don't believe the rubbish you read in comics about them being fierce. That's a lot of nonsense."

Within a couple of days they were flying high over the equatorial rain forest. All the trees were tightly packed together and silver rivers glinted through them like snakes. As they dropped lower, lovely smells wafted up to them from the rich vegetation. It was like drifting over a great, warm oven in which a dozen different cakes were baking.

Down and down they went toward the treetops.

"Well," said Swallow, "this is where I leave you. I hope you children enjoy the rest of the trip."

"Good-bye Swallow, and thank you so much," said Emma.

"See you next year. Save me a place in the barn," called Swallow, as he zoomed off into the distance.

"Now we must go down into the canopy and find those gorillas," said Lancelot.

"What's the canopy?" asked Ivan.

"It's the top layer of the forest," said Lancelot. "It's a world in itself, really. You'll see."

And they did see, for as Belladonna floated downward, a few yards over the tops of the giant trees, it was as if they were progressing through an enchanted, sunlit garden. Everywhere there were flowers and fruit of different colors. The treetops were alive with flocks of brightly colored lizards, tree frogs, squirrels and troops of boisterous monkeys. One troop of monkeys, with white moustaches that made them look rather like Lancelot, climbed on board.

"Have you seen any gorillas?" asked Emma.

"Gorillas?" shrieked one monkey, his mouth full of red fruit.
"No, they live down there where it's dark and hot and horrible.
We live up here where there's plenty of sunshine and nice things
to eat. We wouldn't go down *there*, not even if you offered us a fig
tree full of fruit. We feel sorry for the poor animals who have to
live down there. You could try looking near that big scarlet tree.
The gorillas are sometimes there."

When they got to the scarlet tree, Emma
and the twins were enchanted to see that as
well as being covered with huge red flowers,
the tree was full of sunbirds. These tiny
birds had long, curved beaks and iridescent plumage that made
them gleam like jewels in the sun. They were busy sipping
nectar from the flowers.

"It's like a sort of living Christmas tree," gasped Emma.

"Prettiest birds in Africa," said Lancelot, matter-of-factly.
"Now, come along, we must anchor here and lower the rope
ladder."

"I'll go first," he added, when the silken ladder had been
thrown down, "and fix the end. When I shout, you follow. And
for goodness sake, be careful—it's a long way down. If anyone
falls off, I shall be extremely annoyed."

Lancelot swung himself onto the ladder and started to
descend. It swayed to and fro most alarmingly. Lancelot, it must
be remembered, was no light weight! Just before he disappeared
from view, he missed his footing. The children gasped with
horror, thinking he was going to fall, but luckily he managed to
hold on. In his struggles, though, his sun hat fell off and went
hurtling down to the forest floor. Soon, he vanished after it into
the sea of leaves. Finally, the ladder stopped jerking and the
children knew he had reached the ground safely.

"All fixed. Come down one at a time. Be careful!" he roared.

One by one, the children climbed down cautiously until they
reached the dim light of the forest floor. Conrad was the last to
descend. He stepped off the ladder onto thick leaf-mold, as soft
as a Persian carpet.

"Now," said Lancelot, cleaning his spectacles furiously,
"follow me. Keep close and don't make too much noise."

Walking through the trees, Conrad decided, was rather like
walking through a huge cathedral, only with tree trunks instead
of pillars. It was very hot and still and silent except for the call of
the occasional bird.

After several stops to examine the colorful flowers, he realized
that the others had disappeared. He called to them but there was
no reply. He was all alone and, if he was being honest with
himself, a little bit frightened.

At that moment he saw a movement in the undergrowth. He stepped forward to investigate. A long, black shape reared out of the grass. Startled, Conrad found himself gazing into the glittering eyes of a large, black snake. He tried to speak, but couldn't think quite what to say.

Suddenly, the snake spat at him. Conrad felt a fierce, burning pain on his face and then everything went dark. He couldn't see! Stumbling around blindly, he crashed through some bushes and felt himself falling.

The next thing he heard was Lancelot's voice shouting.

"Over here, please help me!" cried Conrad.

A few minutes later, he felt Lancelot lift him up.

"What on earth happened?" asked Emma, anxiously.

Conrad gasped out his story.

"Spitting cobra," said Lancelot. "Bad-tempered things. But don't worry, the blindness will wear off if we wash your eyes."

They set to work washing Conrad's eyes with Emma's handkerchief and water from the water bottles. Within half an hour, though his eyes were swollen and red, Conrad could see again. Looking around, he realized that in his panic he had fallen down onto a dry riverbed.

Lancelot produced some cheese sandwiches from his pocket and insisted that they should have some lunch and a rest.

After a couple of hours, Conrad felt well enough to continue. They had walked only six hundred and fifty feet when they

heard a noise like a great wave crashing on a beach.

"That's the gorillas moving through the undergrowth," said Lancelot. "I'm glad we've found them at last."

"They—er—sound very big," said Conrad, nervously.

"Even bigger than Lancelot," giggled Ivan.

Suddenly—so suddenly that their hearts almost stopped beating—the bamboos were torn apart and a gigantic gorilla leaped through. He had his mouth open and was banging his chest with his arms. It sounded like someone beating a leather sofa to death with a cricket bat.

"WARRA!" screamed the gorilla. "WARRA ARRAH WARRAAH UGH UGH WARRA UGH UGH UGH."

"OI!" shouted Lancelot above the noise. "Stop all that nonsense. We're friends."

"Oh," said Gorilla, rather taken aback, "are you sure? You look like humans."

"We are," said Emma, "but we won't hurt you. Lancelot's too old and we're too small."

"Well, I suppose you're right," said Gorilla, "but we vegetarians have a terrible time of it, you know. Everyone seems to pick on us and we can't be too careful. It's terribly tiring to have to pretend to be fierce when you're not. You have no idea of the problems it causes."

"Well, you're quite safe with *us*," said Lancelot firmly. "Where is the rest of your family?"

"I'll call them," said Gorilla. "I sent them ahead in case there was trouble."

He uttered a long, roaring, rumbling noise, and presently through the thick undergrowth came three female gorillas, all with babies. On being assured that Lancelot and the children were harmless, the gorilla family gathered around and studied their visitors with interest.

The children had a long and exhausting game of tag with the baby gorillas while Lancelot sat and talked to the old male.

"We're here to look for my brother, Perceval," said Lancelot. "Have you seen him?"

"He was here about two years ago. He was very worried about the destruction of the rain forest, you know," replied Gorilla, warming to his subject. "More and more trees are being chopped down. At this rate there soon won't be any forest left and then what are we animals supposed to do?"

"I don't know what the answer is," said Lancelot, sadly.

"The forest is being felled for timber or to create farmland," continued Gorilla. "It's so thoughtless and stupid. Makes me very angry. You can't replace those great forests once they are gone. Soon we'll have nowhere to live and nothing to eat. This will all be desert and not even humans want that."

"If it's any comfort," said Lancelot, "there are a lot of people in the world who are very concerned and are trying to do something about it. But tell me about Perceval."

"He left and went south to the grasslands around the River Zambesi. He said something about visiting the elephants."

By now the baby gorillas had tired of their game of tag and had found a big patch of wild rhubarb, so the whole family gathered around to feed. As they pulled up the great stems and scrunched them up, they made loud growling noises of satisfaction which sounded almost like distant thunder.

"I think we should slip away quietly and leave the gorillas to their meal," muttered Lancelot to the children.

"But what about Great-Uncle Perceval?" asked Ivan.

"He's gone south to see the elephants," replied Lancelot. "We must follow his trail down to the Zambesi. You can write up your adventures while we're flying there."

CHAPTER THREE

HOT ON THE TRAIL

A few days later, they reached the long, wide, meandering River Zambesi. On its grassy banks, among the clumps of trees, elephants stood in the shade, occasionally spraying themselves with dust. Zebras grazed among the bushes and stately giraffes browsed languidly among the trees. Herds of gnus pirouetted and flicked their heels in mock flight. There were also buffaloes, brown as chocolate, and groups of eland. The children marveled at the sight of so many animals together in the one place.

"We're going down to look for crocodiles," said Lancelot. "They should be lying on the banks now, sunbathing. Get to your telescopes and tell me when you spot one."

The children rushed to their positions and scanned the swampy banks, as Lancelot brought Belladonna down low over the river. The nearest herds of giraffes and antelopes scattered in alarm.

For some time the children saw nothing and were preparing themselves for disappointment, when suddenly Ivan shouted.

"There's one! On the far sandbank."

"Wow," said Conrad. "It's stupendous."

Indeed it was, at least twenty-five feet long, its middle as fat as a truck tire. It was lying in the sun, with its mouth wide open. To the children's amazement, there were two little birds running in and out of its mouth.

"What on earth are they doing?" asked Conrad.

"Whatever they're doing, it looks very dangerous," said Ivan. "I wouldn't like to run in and out of there."

"Nor me," agreed Emma. "Perhaps they're cleaning its teeth."

"Don't be silly!" laughed Conrad.

"She might be right," said Ivan, "Let's go and find out."

Belladonna made a perfect landing. Slowly, the children approached the crocodile.

"Excuse me," said Conrad, boldly. "May we have a word with you?"

The crocodile surveyed them then, very slowly, allowing the plovers to fly away from his teeth, shut his jaws with a snap.

"I really can't spare the time for a chat today," he said. "It's my day for having my teeth cleaned and, since my teeth cleaners come only once a week, they mustn't be interrupted."

"See, I was right!" said Emma.

"Oh, you guessed, did you?" said the crocodile. "How clever. Cleaning my teeth provides food for the plovers and keeps my teeth strong, you see. Now, if you'll excuse me, I really must let them continue. If you want a chat, why not go and talk to my wife? She's over in the reeds, waiting for our babies to hatch. It's boring work and she'll be glad of the company."

The crocodile closed his eyes, opened his mouth again and the two little birds rushed back in. Lancelot and the children made their way over to the reeds. There they came across another huge crocodile. She was lying asleep by a great heap of mud and leaves that was obviously her nest. They paused to look at her vast bulk; but as they were peeping through the reeds, they saw a jackal creeping, silent as a shadow, out of the bushes. He began to dig up the nest.

"Oh, goodness," whispered Emma. "He's going to dig up her eggs. Shouldn't we warn her?"

"He won't get far," said Lancelot. "You watch."

The jackal was so absorbed in his digging that he did not notice the female crocodile slowly open her eyes. Nor did he notice her slowly shift position and stand up on her short, stubby legs.

The next moment, her huge tail flailed around like a giant whip. The jackal was shot high into the air, where he looped the loop three times and came down, with a loud yelp, on his head.

He sat there dazed and whimpering, and the next thing he saw was the crocodile bearing down on him like an express train, her mouth open, uttering ferocious roars. The jackal took one look and fled. The crocodile returned to her nest, lay down and closed her eyes again. The children approached her with caution, amazed at how fast she could move.

"Excuse me," began Emma.

Crocodile opened her eyes and glared.

"Keep away from the nest," she growled. "I have a lot of

trouble with hyenas and vultures after my eggs. How am I expected to cope with humans as well? Keep away, or I'll bite you into small pieces and feed you to the fish."

"We're not after your eggs," Conrad assured her. "Honestly, we're not. We just wanted to learn about crocodiles, and your husband thought you might be glad of a bit of company while you're waiting for your eggs to hatch."

"Did he indeed?" snorted Crocodile in disgust. "It's all right for him, lying on the sandbank all day long having his teeth cleaned, while I guard the nest and ward off scavengers."

She paused for a moment.

"Did you hear something? A sort of squeaking noise?"

The children listened hard.

"Yes," said Emma, who was nearest to the nest. "I heard a squeak. It came from in here."

Crocodile slid forward and started to dig into the nest very carefully. Slowly, she uncovered a pile of white eggs. The top one had a hole in it and the children could see something moving inside. Other eggs cracked and the squeaking grew louder.

Gradually the hole in the top egg grew bigger and a baby crocodile poked his head out. He had a squat little nose, rather like a duck's beak. His curved mouth seemed to be smiling with delight at his arrival in the world.

He struggled out of the egg and then, to the children's astonishment, the mother crocodile opened her huge jaws, showing her monstrous, sharp teeth, and picked the baby up. She lumbered down to the water, put him in the safety of the reeds and came back to the nest, where more baby crocodiles were emerging thick and fast.

"Can we help?" pleaded Emma, who longed to pick one up.

"Thank you," said Crocodile, "that would be most kind."

Lancelot and the children gathered up the baby crocodiles and carried them down to the river. They had to be very careful because the little teeth could nip quite fiercely.

Presently, all forty babies were safely clustered in the reeds with their mother lying in the water guarding them. Then Emma asked Crocodile a few more questions, writing the answers carefully into the diary.

"Age, fifty . . . Husband, ninety-four . . . hopes to live to over a hundred. Gosh! Total number of children, unknown . . . let me see, fifty times forty is . . . Wow! Length, twenty feet . . . Maximum time under water . . . forty-five MINUTES! Fantastic!" By the time Emma had finished, her head was spinning.

Finally tiring of answering questions, Crocodile swam off, with her babies swimming after her. Emma thought she looked rather like a duck followed by her ducklings.

Each of the children took an empty egg shell as a souvenir and wandered back to Belladonna.

"We'll fly on tomorrow," suggested Lancelot, "find a water hole and land. Then we can talk to the elephants and ask about Perceval."

"Oh great!" said Emma. "Another animal for the diary."

The following afternoon they landed Belladonna behind the acacia trees surrounding a large water hole. As they neared the pool, they heard an excited "Churr, churr". A small, brown bird with white cheeks and a yellow patch on his wings flew into a tree above them.

"Stop," whispered Lancelot, "that's a honey guide. Now we shall see some fun. Any minute now, honey badgers will arrive."

The bird called again and suddenly out of the long grass appeared two animals. They had long, low bodies like big dachshunds, with stumpy legs, blunt faces and short tails.

"Come on, come on," shouted the little bird. It flew a little farther and then perched on an acacia tree with a large hole in it. "Churr, churr. Come on. Not a moment to lose."

"Why are they called honey badgers?" whispered Ivan, not wanting to disturb the creatures as they sniffed around the bottom of the tree.

"Because they love honey," replied Lancelot, watching the honey badgers climb the tree. "They will eat other things — grasshoppers, birds' eggs, mice, rats, lizards, even snakes." Conrad shivered, remembering the spitting cobra. "But it's honey they love best."

"Oh, do hurry up, it'll be dark soon," screamed the honey guide impatiently.

"But what are the badgers and the bird doing together?" asked Emma.

"Well, bees build their nests high in the trees. Honey badgers are too near the ground to spot them. So the honey guide spots the nests and leads the badgers there," replied Lancelot.

"They work together, you mean? Hey, that's rather like the plover and the crocodile," said Emma excitedly, pulling out the diary.

"So the honey guide must get something out of it," said Ivan thoughtfully.

"Well done indeed," said Lancelot, looking very pleased. "You *are* keeping your wits about you. Yes, the honey guide wants the honey badgers to break open the bees' nest so it can eat the wax and the baby bees."

"But surely wax would give it indigestion," protested Conrad.

"The honey guide has a special tiny organism that lives in its tummy," Lancelot explained. "That organism eats the wax and turns it into fatty acids which the bird can digest."

"Fantastic," said Emma. The twins nodded in agreement.

They all watched the honey badgers tearing off the rotten wood around the entrance to the beehive. A great cloud of angry bees emerged but, undaunted, the honey badgers dug on. They threw honeycombs to the ground, some containing honey and others containing baby bees.

"Their thick fur stops them from being stung," guessed Ivan. Lancelot nodded.

The honey guide seemed beside himself with joy, prodding out the baby bees from the wax. But just as the two honey badgers were starting to descend the tree to feast on the honey, Lancelot gave a great roar. The children jumped in surprise and the poor honey badgers fell out of their tree.

"Wah, wah, ouch, they're stinging me!" Lancelot screamed, whirling around and around. "HELP! They're stinging me!"

Then slapping himself and yelling, he set off through the trees at a ponderous gallop. Swarming around his head was a huge cloud of angry bees.

"Quick," said Emma, "let's go after him before he gets into trouble."

Lancelot was too fat to be able to run very fast. The children overtook him just as he burst through the trees by the pool. Antelopes, zebras and gnus scattered in panic as Lancelot roared by. A herd of elephants, startled by his sudden appearance, wheeled to face him, fanning out their ears aggressively.

"Friend, friend! OUCH!" he shouted desperately. Then, unable to stop, he ran straight through the middle of the surprised elephants and dived head first into the water.

The elephants stared at Lancelot's sun hat as it bobbed on the water. The bees circled for a minute then, frustrated, they buzzed back toward their nest.

Lancelot rose to the surface, snorting like a hippopotamus.

"I must apologize," he spluttered, addressing a huge cow elephant who seemed to be the leader of the herd. "I'm so sorry for interrupting your evening bath, but my life was being threatened by thousands of bees."

"I forgive you, Lancelot," said Elephant. "Bees must be very troublesome to slow-moving creatures with thin skins."

"How do you know who I am?" asked Lancelot.

"Your brother, Perceval, described you in great detail," replied Elephant, casually flicking a trunkful of dust over her shoulders. "Especially that peculiar sun hat."

"Excellent," said Lancelot eagerly. "Where is he? We've come all the way from England to find him."

"He left here just under two years ago. But I'm afraid I don't know where he went," apologized Elephant.

"Oh, no!" exploded Lancelot. "That's just like Perceval not to leave a forwarding address. He *must* have said something. Can't you remember *anything?*"

"Well, he did talk about a duckbilled platypus," Elephant said after a moment's thought. "Whatever that is."

Lancelot sighed, sat down and started to wring out his clothes.

"I suppose you're scientists, like Perceval?" inquired Elephant, turning to the children.

"Not exactly," replied Emma, hauling out the diary, "but we would like to ask you some questions."

"Yes, just like Perceval," Elephant nodded wearily. "Why don't you climb up and measure me instead?"

Conrad stood on Ivan's shoulders but couldn't reach Elephant's back. Suddenly a soft rubbery trunk curled around them both and lifted them up. They shouted down to Emma unscientific measurements such as "Over two doors high . . . ears as big as dinner tables . . . tough skin." Emma sketched and wrote furiously, trying to keep up.

"That's enough," said Elephant. "Come on, I'll give you all a ride."

Emma was lifted up to join the twins. Before moving off, Elephant trumpeted softly. Out of the herd staggered a baby elephant, about the size of a goat and covered with long, rusty-colored hair.

"My new baby," said Elephant, proudly. The baby elephant trotted along happily behind its mother.

"Careful now," cried Lancelot. "Don't go far!"

By the time Elephant brought Emma and the twins back from their ride, the other animals, realizing that Lancelot and the children were friends, had come back to the water hole to drink.

There was a lot of bickering among the gnus. "If you push me again you'll get my horn in your ribs," said one to the other.

The elands were scarcely better behaved and one or two occasionally bit or kicked their companions.

The giraffes straddled their front legs wide so that they could bend their long necks and get their heads down in the water. Having drunk their fill, they stood about and discussed the various flavors of the acacia trees they had been feeding on during the day. It sounded almost like a cooking class.

"A mouthful of the tiny leaves from the top of that tree, mixed slowly with a few of the bigger leaves is delicious," said one.

"I like to put a tiny bit of bark with the leaves, it makes all the difference," suggested another.

The children soon lost interest in this rather tedious conversation and looked around to see what else was going on.

"Look! Over there!" pointed Ivan, in excitement. "Lions!"

Following Ivan's gaze, Emma and Conrad saw a huge black-maned lion appearing through the acacias, followed by his two wives and five cubs. Slowly, the lion family ambled down to the water's edge and started to drink. Although the lions were very close to the other creatures, the antelopes and elands took no notice of them.

"Why, if they run away from us, don't they run away from the lions?" Emma wondered.

"Because they know the lions are well-fed," explained Elephant, spraying water from her trunk over her baby's head. "If the lions hadn't been well-fed, you wouldn't have seen those antelopes for dust."

When they had drunk enough, the lion and lionesses lay down on the bank. The cubs gamboled about, stalking each other, having wrestling matches and occasionally leaping on top of their father and biting his tail, much to his annoyance.

"That's the way they learn how to hunt," observed Ivan.

"I must say, their father looks very noble," said Emma, busily sketching him in the diary.

"Well, he may *look* noble," said Elephant. "But I assure you he's not."

"But he's called the King of Beasts," retorted Emma.

"Nonsense!" snorted Elephant. "If he's a king, he's a pretty poor one. At the first sign of trouble he disappears and lets his wives take care of it."

"Well, I don't believe you," Emma said, fiercely. "I think you're making it up."

"No, she's right," agreed Lancelot, who had been busy examining his bee stings.

"You mean," asked Conrad, "that all these great, fierce lions we hear about are really cowards?"

"Well, I suppose you could say that," replied Lancelot. "On the other hand, in the animal kingdom, females often do the important work. It seems to suit the lions all right. Now look here, you children, could you please do something about these bee stings? They hurt dreadfully."

"Well, we can't do anything here!" said Emma. "We'll need to go back to Belladonna and see what's in the medicine chest."

"Perhaps we ought to get back," she sighed regretfully. "Anyway, it looks as if it's going to get dark soon."

At that moment a large rhinoceros trotted out of the acacias and rumbled toward the pool.

"Hang on, here's someone new to talk to," said Conrad.

"I would keep away from him," advised Elephant. "Rhinos have bad eyesight and are very bad-tempered. Their motto seems to be *Charge first and ask questions later.*"

"Quite so," said Lancelot, irritably, "but I flatter myself that I have the wit and diplomacy to handle any creature, however impatient its nature. I've dealt with pythons, vampire bats and sharks. I'm not going to be frightened by a mere rhino."

"Well, I wouldn't go near that one," Elephant advised. "He seems in a foul temper."

"We'll see," replied Lancelot. "I shall go and have a few words with him, man to man." And off he waddled, rubbing his bee stings, to where the rhino was drinking.

"I don't think he's being very sensible," said Emma, anxiously.

"I agree with you," said Elephant. "My advice is to start back to your balloon at once. It'll save a lot of running later on."

The children said good-bye
and started back to Belladonna.

"Good-bye and good luck,"
trumpeted Elephant.

"May I have a word with you,
my good rhino?" called Lancelot,
drawing nearer. Rhino wheeled around. Lancelot stopped. They
peered at each other short-sightedly.

"I was just wondering, my good rhino . . ." Lancelot began.

"How dare you interrupt my drink? You wait till I get my horn
into you!" snorted Rhino, and charged.

Lancelot turned and ran toward the children, shouting over his
shoulder, "Now don't be so silly, I'm your friend."

The children, seeing Lancelot and Rhino bearing down on
them, began to run as fast as they could toward Belladonna.

Fortunately, Rhino was delayed by digging his horn into a fat
tree, mistakenly thinking it was Lancelot. This gave them all
time to get on board and raise the anchors. As Belladonna floated
upward, Rhino freed himself and charged again.

"Filthy cowards," he roared, "flying away from a fight!"

"There you are," announced Lancelot, wiping his brow. "I
told you. Nothing to it. All it needed was a bit of diplomacy."

The children looked at each other, then started to giggle.

"Now stop all that," said Lancelot, severely, "and get up to
the flight deck. We must have a council of war."

Once on the flight deck, Lancelot took out some large maps and spread them on his desk.

"Now," he said, turning to the children. "I know where Perceval has gone."

"But how?" asked Ivan. "Elephant said she didn't know."

"Ah, yes," nodded Lancelot, "but she also mentioned that he was interested in the duckbilled platypus. Now that creature is found in only one place—Australia."

"Australia!" the children gasped. "But that's thousands and thousands of miles away."

"Belladonna can fly twice that distance," said Lancelot. "I built her, after all. I should know. We've got plenty of supplies and we'll fill the water tanks tomorrow. But what about you? Do you want to go on?" he asked.

"Oh, yes," they chorused. "Yes, please!"

"Very well. Just remember, the special powder lets you communicate with animals but it doesn't protect you from them. You must be much more careful than you have been today. Now stop laughing and attend to my bee stings. Do you want me to die of blood poisoning, you unfeeling lot?"

CHAPTER FOUR

SIDETRACKED IN THE OUTBACK

The day was doubly exciting. In the first place, Belladonna had made the voyage from Africa without a hitch. The strong trade winds, which used to drive the old sailing ships, had carried her safely to the great Red Desert of Australia. She was now anchored close to Ayers Rock. Lancelot told them that, at one thousand feet high and five-and-a-half miles around, this was the biggest single rock in the world.

All around them the landscape shimmered in the heat. What little vegetation they could see was burned brown by the sun.

The second reason for excitement was that it was the twins' birthday. They were all looking forward to a birthday picnic in the cool of the evening near Ayers Rock. They wanted to watch the spectacular sunset, which Lancelot assured them was one of the best in the world.

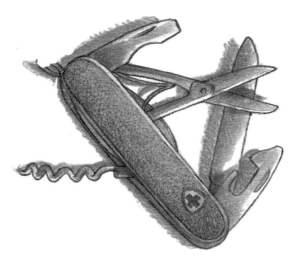

The twins opened their presents before lunch. Lancelot gave each of them a bright red Swiss army knife. These had several blades, and bristled with useful gadgets—scissors, tweezers, corkscrews, saws and even a compass. They were really several presents in one. The twins were speechless with pleasure.

"Most useful for explorers," said Lancelot gruffly.

Emma gave the twins a hand-telescope each. The ones on the flight deck were too heavy for them to carry around. Ivan and Conrad both wanted to try out the telescopes at once, but Emma reminded them that the birthday picnic had to be prepared.

Lancelot had already made a special cake full of dried fruit. The smell from the oven was delicious. Deciding he had done enough, he went off to have a bath. Emma and the twins made a mountain of sandwiches, using cucumbers grown in the garden.

The children then did their chores. They collected the spiders' webs. They watered the fruit trees and the mushrooms. Conrad and Ivan fed the electric eels with frozen goldfish.

Then they went up to the veranda, to gaze at Ayers Rock and to escape from the strains of "Waltzing Matilda" which were floating loudly from the bathroom.

"What's that burning smell?" asked Conrad, sniffing loudly. Emma uttered a scream of dismay and fled down to the kitchen. She was just in time. The top of the cake was about to turn from brown to black. Lancelot was enjoying himself so much in the bath that he had forgotten all about it.

When Lancelot finally emerged from the bathroom, they packed the picnic hamper.

Then they climbed out onto the warm white sand. They walked through the tough spinifex grass, past little clumps of eucalyptus trees toward the rock. It looked gigantic in the early evening sun.

"Now," said Lancelot, spreading out the cloth, "let's get on with the party. Pass the cucumber sandwiches."

The party was a great success and the cake, saved from disaster, was perfect. The twins, with a single giant puff, blew out all the candles. They were just wiping the crumbs from their mouths when Lancelot pointed toward the eucalyptus scrub.

"Look," he said excitedly, "a marsupial mouse."

There, in among the spinifex tussocks, was a small brown creature bouncing toward them like a ball.

"Marsupial? Do you mean to say that it's got a pouch like a kangaroo?" asked Conrad in surprise.

"Yes. All animals in Australia have pouches, except the ones imported by humans," explained Lancelot.

By this time the marsupial mouse had bounded quite close to them and they could hear her panting and talking to herself.

"Oh dear, what shall I do? My poor babies. There's nowhere to hide. I shall be caught. Oh dear, my poor babies."

"Excuse me," said Emma, leaning forward and calling gently. "We're friends. Can we help you?"

"Eeeeek," screamed Mouse, leaping about three feet in the air, turning a somersault and landing in a flurry of sand, where she sat, quivering with fright.

"Oh, please," said Emma, distressed, "don't be frightened, we only want to help. What's the problem?"

"I've been pursued by a vicious dingo for over an hour. Please hide me," begged Mouse in a shaking voice.

Quick as a flash, Emma scooped a hole in the sand. She popped Mouse into it and put the cake plate on top.

"Brilliant," said the twins.

"Now, let's behave as if nothing had happened," said Lancelot, trying to look innocent.

The dingo suddenly appeared at a brisk trot, ears pricked and nose to the ground. His fur shone yellow as honey in the rays of the setting sun. He saw them and stopped.

"We're friends," Lancelot called. "Come and join us."

Dingo, reassured, trotted over and sat near the cake.

"G'day. Who are you then?" asked Dingo.

"Travelers, just travelers," replied Lancelot airily.

"Have a slice of birthday cake," offered Emma politely.

"No thanks," said Dingo. "I'm after a juicy mouse. Have you seen one go past lately?"

"Why yes, we *have* seen a mouse," replied Emma.

Lancelot and the twins stared at her, astonished and horrified.

"You mean a small, marsupial mouse?" Emma went on.

"That's her," said Dingo, showing his teeth.

"She went that way," said Emma, pointing into the distance.

"How long ago was that?" asked Dingo, saliva trickling out of the side of his mouth in anticipation of a meal.

"Only a minute or so," said Emma. "She seemed very tired. I expect you'll catch up with her easily."

"No worries. I sure will," growled Dingo and bounded off.

"Quick work," said Lancelot. "Excellent, Emma."

After Dingo had gone, Emma lifted the plate.

"Thank you for saving me," squeaked Mouse, creeping out.

She was very pretty. She sat up on her slender hind legs like a miniature kangaroo as she talked to them.

"I'm glad we were able to help," said Lancelot. "Dingoes are not my favorite animals."

"Nor mine," said Mouse, shuddering.

"Could we see your babies, please?" asked Emma.

"Certainly," said Mouse. Hopping close to them, she pulled open her pouch. Inside lay ten baby mice, peering up at them with big, dark eyes. Each one was no bigger than the last joint of Emma's little finger.

"Aren't they adorable?" said Emma, as she gently stroked the velvety babies. Mouse drank the milk they offered her, then said good-bye and bounced off in the opposite direction from Dingo. She soon disappeared into the shadows.

Lancelot and the children sat on, watching the sun go down and the moon rising from behind Ayers Rock. They were fascinated by the way the rock changed color. It went red, purple, yellow, green, blue and finally black.

The twins voted it the best birthday they had ever had. Sleepily, they boarded Belladonna and sailed off southward.

In the morning when they awoke, they were astonished to find
Belladonna anchored in a small clearing in a thick eucalyptus
forest. Lancelot was nowhere to be seen.

Emma and the twins were worried. He had never disappeared
before without telling them where he was going.

"Let's organize a search party," suggested Emma.

She wrote a note in case Lancelot returned while they were
away. The twins packed a survival backpack. They put in four
water bottles, salt tablets, the first aid kit, a coil of rope and a
bag of sandwiches. Each of them carried a shiny piece of metal
and a whistle for signaling. The boys took their new telescopes
and knives.

"I knew these would come in useful," said Ivan. "We can cut
notches in trees to mark our trail."

Conrad produced a big sheet of clear plastic and an empty tin
which he packed in the backpack.

"It's for a solar still," he explained in a superior tone. "It's a
clever way of collecting water in deserts."

Finally, remembering to take their sun hats, they set out.

They marked their trail carefully and every ten minutes one of
the twins climbed a tree to look through his telescope. Using the
compasses, they worked out a proper search pattern. They
shouted loudly but there was no reply. It was a very scientific and
efficient search, but there was no sign of Lancelot. Emma was
starting to get really worried when Ivan shouted.

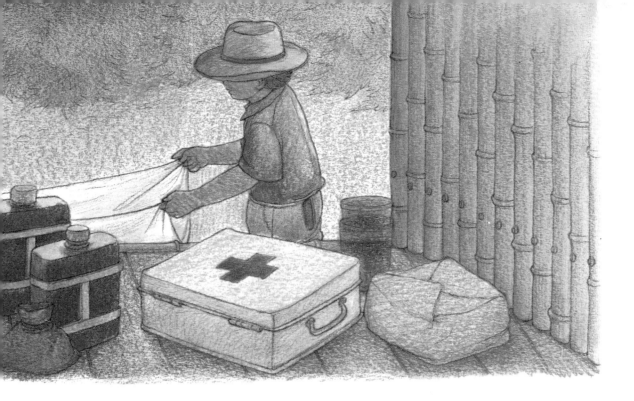

"I can see something ahead."

They ran forward and were horrified to see Lancelot lying face down in the bushes.

"Lancelot, are you all right?" panted Emma.

Lancelot turned over and glared at them.

"I'm fine apart from the headache you've given me with all your shouting. I just came out to watch the mallee fowl."

"But we've come to rescue you," said Conrad.

"I don't need rescuing," said Lancelot in surprise.

"Well, we didn't know that," said the twins. "You might have fallen down a precipice. You didn't tell us where you had gone, so how were we to know?"

"You're quite right," said Lancelot guiltily. "I might have gone and broken my ankle or something. I should have told you all, but I had a surprise for you. I wanted to make sure that the surprise was there before you saw it, d'you see?"

"We understand," said Emma, then added severely, "but please don't do it again. It gave us all a shock."

"I won't, I promise," said Lancelot, humbly.

"Well, what's the surprise?" asked Conrad, eagerly.

"Yes, come on, tell us," said Ivan.

"Look," said Lancelot, pointing through the bushes. In the center of a clearing was a huge mound and around it were lots of scratch marks as though something had been piling up the earth.

"Now what do you think that is?" he asked.

"A lot of mud," said Emma.

"Wrong," said Lancelot, triumphantly. "It's an incubator for hatching eggs—and here comes the owner and builder."

Through the trees walked a beautiful bird, the size of a turkey. It was every color of brown you could imagine.

"That's the incubator builder, the mallee fowl," said Lancelot.

The mallee fowl walked up to the nest, stuck his open beak into it then scraped some sand off the top. This action was repeated until the mallee fowl seemed satisfied.

"Well, any guesses as to what he's doing?" asked Lancelot.

"Is he checking to see that the eggs are all right?" asked Emma.

"No," said Lancelot. "Not a bad guess, but no. Try again."

"Is he checking the temperature?" suggested Ivan.

"And scraping off sand to cool it down!" added Ivan, trying to make it seem as if this had been his idea too.

"Yes, well done! He's using his mouth as a thermometer," Lancelot explained, as the amazed Emma wrote busily in the diary. "You see, the nest is made of rotting vegetation which makes the inside hot, like a compost heap. The sand keeps the heat in."

"How long does it take to build?" asked Emma.

"Why not ask the mallee fowl," suggested Lancelot.

After the introductions had been made, Mallee Fowl told them that he had begun digging the hole for the nest in winter. It had taken four months to prepare the nest before his wives were satisfied that it was the right temperature for them to lay their eggs.

"I've spent the last six months guarding the eggs and keeping the temperature correct," he added proudly.

"What tremendous work," said Emma. "You must be exhausted."

"I am," said Mallee Fowl, "but it's worth it. Look there."

They looked at the nest. The sand was starting to move and trickle down the side. The tip of the beak, head and finally the whole body of a baby mallee fowl emerged. It rested awhile, panting, then ran off into the forest.

"Don't you look after it?" asked Emma, surprised.

"No," said Mallee Fowl, proudly, "as soon as our babies hatch, they can look after themselves."

"It's wonderful," said Emma. "Thanks so much for showing us. What luck we arrived when we did."

Mallee Fowl gave them some of his feathers as souvenirs. They left him standing on his nest and returned to Belladonna.

"Now," said Lancelot, poring over a map, "we're off to see the duckbilled platypus, if I can work out how to get there. With luck, we should be there tomorrow evening."

Lancelot managed to work out their route—with a little bit of
help from Ivan and Conrad, who were becoming very efficient
map readers. By late afternoon on the next day, Belladonna
landed on the grassy banks of a brown, slow-moving river, just on
the edge of a huge eucalyptus forest. Some of the trees had
green and silver bark and silvery-green leaves, while others had
white trunks and green leaves. The white trunks looked as
though somebody had written all over the bark with a black pen.

Lancelot explained that these were called scribblegums, for all eucalyptus trees are called gum trees in Australia. The children decided to take some peeling bark as souvenirs. Lancelot left them to their task and, feeling very hot, waded into the river in an effort to cool down.

As the children were pulling off strips with good scribble marks, they heard a voice addressing them from above—a furry, slow sort of voice.

"What are you doing, pulling my tree to pieces?" inquired the voice.

The children looked up and there, perched in the branches of the trees around them, were several sleepy-looking koalas.

"I beg your pardon," said Emma to the biggest koala, who had spoken to them. "We weren't pulling it to pieces, we were just peeling off some of the dried bark to take home with us."

"Oh well, if that's all you were doing, go ahead, but eucalyptus trees are very important to us, you know," said Koala, scratching his thick fur thoughtfully.

"I know," said Conrad. "You eat the leaves, don't you?"

"Yes, we do," said Koala, enthusiastically. "It's the only thing we do eat, really. We can't eat anything else."

"I think it must taste like cough medicine," whispered Ivan.

"Me too," said Conrad. "Horrid! Ugh!"

"Well, don't say so," whispered Emma, "or you'll insult them."

"Tell me something," said Lancelot to Koala. "Did you know that at certain times of the year the young leaves and shoots of a certain type of eucalyptus contain a deadly poison?"

"Of course," said Koala, casually. "We just don't eat that

particular kind of tree during that period."

"But how do you know when it's poisonous?" asked Lancelot.

"We just do," yawned Koala, as if bored with the conversation.

"I wonder," asked Emma, "would you be kind enough to let us have a photo of you all with one of us holding your babies?"

"Certainly," replied Koala, amiably, and the whole family descended from the trees and climbed onto the children until they were weighed down with koalas on their backs, heads and shoulders and even hanging onto their arms and legs.

Lancelot took the photographs and made a great fuss about getting them right. Then he took one of Conrad holding two adorable babies. They thanked the koalas warmly and walked on farther down the river.

They had gone a half mile or so when suddenly they saw, grazing among the trees, a group of red kangaroos. As they approached, the leader reared up on his hind legs.

The children were amazed at how tall he was—even taller than Lancelot. Kangaroo stared at them with a superior expression.

"What might I do for you?" he asked in a schoolmastery voice.

"Gosh," said Emma, rather in awe of him. "Perhaps you could

tell us something about yourself?'' she stammered.

"Of course," said Kangaroo. "There are fifty-one kinds of kangaroos—the great gray kangaroos; the wallabies and rock wallabies, they're much smaller than we, of course; hare wallabies and rat kangaroos, they're smaller still; tree kangaroos who, naturally enough, live in trees. . . ."

"Good grief," interrupted Emma, hastily, "I never realized there were so many different kinds."

"Could we have a look at some of your babies?" asked Ivan, before Kangaroo could start again.

"Certainly," said Kangaroo. He grunted an order and three female kangaroos kindly hopped forward.

Inside the first female's fur-lined pouch lay a pink, new-born baby, no bigger than a bean.

"Why, it's tiny!" cried Emma.

"It's blind at that age and can only use its front limbs," said Lancelot. "Yet when it's born it can climb from its mother's tail and find its way into her pouch."

The second female's baby, though still pink and hairless, was older and looked much more like a kangaroo.

The third female hopped forward, her pouch bulging. Out poked the baby's head, its ears pricked and eyes bright. It was a smaller version of its parents, with red fur and a long tail. It struggled out of the pouch. Ivan stroked it gently.

"Now . . ." began Kangaroo, taking a deep breath.

The twins looked at each other and groaned.

"The habits of the wallaby . . . ," began Kangaroo. ". . . That's odd, where is everybody?"

There was no answer. Lancelot and the children had crept away.

The sun was about to set and the eucalyptus forest cast long, black shadows as the sky turned gold, then green. The children heard something splash out of the water and onto the bank.

"What on earth is it?" wondered Emma.

"It looks like Donald Duck," whispered Ivan.

"Donald Duck in a fur coat," said Conrad.

"Wrong," laughed Lancelot. "*This* is the duckbilled platypus."

Platypus stopped chomping on what looked like a hose but was actually an Australian giant worm and looked around at them.

"Have a piece of worm," he offered kindly.

"No thanks," said Emma, repressing a shudder, "not just now."

"Suit yourself," said Platypus, "but you're refusing a treat, I can tell you, because this is a particularly delicious one."

"Do you eat many worms?" asked Ivan.

"Not a lot," replied Platypus, casually. "About a pound a day. I also eat half a pound of shrimps and beetle grubs plus an odd fish and frog. Now it's my turn to ask a question," he continued. "It's a riddle. Why is a platypus like six animals and yet like no other animal at all?"

"You're like a duck with your webbed feet and beak," said Ivan.

"Your fur is like a mole's," offered Conrad.

"You've got a beaver's tail," Lancelot chipped in.

"That's three," giggled Platypus. "Give up?"

There was silence as they all looked at the curious creature.

"All right then, here's a clue," Platypus preened himself. "The other animals are a cow, a bird and a snake."

The children still couldn't work it out and Lancelot refused to help. Platypus looked at them triumphantly.

"I win," he cheered. "I feed my babies with milk, like the cow, but like the bird, I lay eggs. My spurs carry poison like a snake and I think you'll agree that makes me like no other animal in the world."

"Yes, you really are a puzzle," agreed Emma.

"Not just a puzzle. The first scientists who saw us thought we were a joke. My great-great-great-great-grandfather's skin was sent to London. Well, they wouldn't believe it. They thought it was lots of different animals all sewn together. Can you imagine it? Ho, ho, ho. My great-great-great-great-grandfather must have been very annoyed, them not believing in him!" laughed Platypus, rolling about in the grass and holding his sides. "Tee-hee, tee-hee, tee-hee."

When everyone had finished laughing, Lancelot asked Platypus about Perceval.

"Oh, yes," said Platypus, wiping tears of mirth from his eyes. "We had a very jolly time indeed. But I'm afraid he left about eighteen months ago. He told me he was going to study polar bears at the North Pole."

"Well, children," said Lancelot, looking very serious. "This means a very long voyage indeed. We'd better get back to Belladonna at once, and prepare for a trip to the frozen north. You'll need to get out your winter clothes!"

They were sorry to leave the amusing platypus, but giving the kangaroos a wide berth, they returned to Belladonna.

CHAPTER FIVE

THE TRAIL GOES COLD

Lancelot was standing on the flight deck, wearing his radio earphones and frowning fiercely. Presently, he took the earphones off and looked at the children.

"Hurricane, dead ahead," he said gravely. "We should go down and anchor, but according to the charts there's nothing around here for us to anchor on. Not an island for over fifty miles in any direction. This is very serious. I don't know what to do."

They were more than halfway across the Pacific Ocean and during the last few days had passed over hundreds of little islands with snow-white beaches. Now, when they needed an island most, there was not a single one they could reach in time. Already the blue sky was streaked with black clouds and the wind was so fierce that the bamboo house was creaking and groaning alarmingly.

"All hands to batten down the hatches," Lancelot ordered. The children rushed about obeying his order. Lancelot seemed cheerful enough but the children realized that he was worried. They had to get Belladonna lower or the hurricane would rip the balloon apart.

While the children were discussing this dreadful possibility in hushed voices, Lancelot scanned the horizon. Suddenly, he stiffened, then uttered a triumphant "Hah!"

He disappeared inside and soon they felt Belladonna dropping toward the sea.

"There's a blue whale with a baby over there," said Lancelot, when he reemerged. "She might help us. We'll see."

The children rushed to the telescope. Below them they saw the huge, shining backs of a whale and her baby wallowing in the white-topped waves churned up by the hurricane. Carefully, Lancelot maneuvered Belladonna until she was nearly touching the sea.

"Ahoy!" shouted Lancelot through his megaphone. "Ahoy, Blue Whale. Can you help us?"

Blue Whale surveyed them with a large glittering eye.

"Who are you?" she asked, her voice sounding as rich and throbbing as a whole orchestra.

"Just harmless travelers," explained Lancelot. "We *must* land or we will be destroyed by the hurricane. Could we, by any chance, use your back as a landing place?"

"Use my back?" snorted Whale, blowing a fountain of water over the children and Lancelot. "What nerve!"

"Look," said Lancelot, desperately, wiping the water off his spectacles with a purple-and-yellow handkerchief. "I didn't mean to be so insulting, truly, it's just that there are no islands around here and you're so marvelously big and strong and brave that we thought you might tow us."

"My, my," said Whale, flattered. "Big and strong and brave, you say? Of course I'll help. What had you in mind?"

"If you took a big loop of rope in your mouth," said Lancelot, climbing down the ladder, "you could anchor us and tow us too."

With their hearts in their mouths the children watched Lancelot, bobbing around on the end of the ladder, trying to throw the rope to the whale while the wind, which blew more and more fiercely, kept snatching it away. At last, just when they had almost given up hope, Whale caught it in her mouth and turned to pull the balloon.

Unfortunately, Ivan, anxious to see what was happening, had been standing peering over the edge of the veranda, his foot on the rope. As it pulled tight, he lost his balance and was catapulted into the sea below.

"Man overboard!" yelled Lancelot at the top of his voice. Emma and Conrad turned pale and clutched each other.

"Help!" they chorused. "Oh, Whale, please help!"

But Whale was so busy pulling Belladonna and keeping her steady that she didn't seem to hear. Whatever were they going to do?

Just then, the baby whale caught sight of Ivan bobbing up and down in the giant waves. Straightaway he turned and dived. A few seconds later he rose under Ivan and lifted him right out of the water on his back. Lancelot, wobbling on the very bottom of the rope ladder, reached out for Ivan. He grabbed him by the collar and helped him back onto Belladonna.

Ivan stood dripping like a drowned rat. He was very shaken by his adventure, so Lancelot sent him off at once to change his clothes and have some hot soup.

"From now on, we all wear safety lines," Lancelot announced, firmly.

For three days and three nights they were pulled along by their trusty friend, while the wind howled around them and the rain

lashed Belladonna. The children kept warm inside.

The twins sorted out their photographs, while Emma tidied up the diary, especially the places which had been hurriedly written. She began a new section headed "The Blue Whale". In this she wrote down all the information she gathered from shouted conversations with the whales whenever the wind dropped.

Emma was so pleased with her work that she celebrated by cooking pancakes for everyone. She had no trouble cooking the pancakes, but tossing them proved extremely tricky. Belladonna was swinging to and fro like a pendulum, so most of the pancakes landed on the floor or on the furniture. One actually landed on Lancelot's head. He was not at all pleased and said so in no uncertain terms. But even he had to admit that the pancakes were delicious, and soon there was not a single one left.

On the fourth morning they woke up and for a moment could not think what was wrong. They realized that there was no wind and Belladonna was sailing along steadily. Hurriedly they dressed and rushed up onto the veranda. The sky was clear and the sea was calm, as if such things as hurricanes did not exist.

Lancelot was hanging over the rail, talking to Whale.

"Hullo, you children," he greeted them. "We're in luck here. Whale is heading for the same part of the Arctic as we are and has offered to show us the quickest way of getting there."

"Wonderful," said Emma. "You are kind."

"Not at all, not at all," fluted Whale. "We travelers must help each other. You're lucky to have met me, actually. I was delayed by my baby being ill, otherwise I'd be out there already. I'm so hungry, I can't wait to get among all those tasty shrimps in the northern seas."

"How long will it take us to get there?" asked Conrad.

"About another week," said Whale, "if the weather holds good."

For the next week they followed in the foamy track of the whale. The voyage was fascinating. They passed a troop of dolphins who were so full of high spirits that it was all Emma could do to make them stay still for an interview.

A flying fish flew on board by mistake and Emma had to interview him very quickly, so as to put him back in the sea before he suffocated.

Day by day the weather got colder.

"Time to look in the trunk," said Lancelot and led them into one of the little storerooms on the ground floor. The children were amazed by the huge selection of winter clothes that Lancelot had brought. They delved into the heap and chose bright red flannel underwear, thick trousers, lamb's wool sweaters, woolly hats and big boots lined with musk-ox fur.

"Now to prepare Belladonna for the cold," said Lancelot. Extra musk-ox insulation was put around the doors and windows to keep out the drafts. The electric eels were given

double rations to boost the heating. Lancelot took special care with the garden. The spiders were set to work spinning thin but warm webs over the trees to keep out the cold. Even though it was getting colder outside, Belladonna was as warm as toast.

Then came the great morning when they went up onto the veranda and there, all around them, huge snowfields lay glittering in the sun. The wind had blown the snow so that it looked as if it had been plowed.

There were enormous cracks in the brilliant blue ice and here and there big icebergs had broken away and were sailing along majestically, pushed by the wind. They were all sorts of shapes and sizes. They changed color like rainbows as the sun caught them. Some had ice caves that looked dark and mysterious.

Presently, to the children's astonishment, the deep blue sea turned quite pink. Lancelot explained that this was where the krill shrimps congregated. Millions of their tiny pink bodies colored the water. Here Whale left them and took her baby off to have a shrimp feast.

Belladonna flew on and presently Lancelot landed her on the ice. Though it was cold, the sun was hot and so the children didn't know whether to take clothes off or keep them on. They went out onto the ice field and followed Lancelot to a spot a hundred feet from the balloon.

"Now," asked Lancelot, "do you know where you are?"

"Yes," replied Emma, excitedly, "the North Pole."

Gathering around the spot, they planted two banners which the twins had made to show other explorers that the Dollybutt Expedition had been there.

"Now," said Lancelot as they took off again and sailed southward, "it's time to look for polar bears. Keep an eye out for seals, they always know the whereabouts of polar bears."

They sailed low over the ice floes and deep blue Polar Sea.

"Aha," said Lancelot, presently. "There you are, there's a school of killer whales. Nice friendly chaps, in spite of their name. We'll go and ask them. They're sure to know."

They landed and walked toward the edge of the ice floe, their boots squeaking in the snow like mice. The killer whales, their handsome black-and-white bodies gleaming in the sun, were swimming to and fro some sixty-five feet from the edge of the ice floe. As they approached, Lancelot paused and filled his lungs, ready to give the whales a shout when, to his annoyance, the whole school suddenly dived beneath the surface and disappeared.

"Drat," said Lancelot, irritably. "That's the worst thing about killer whales. They spend so much time beneath the water you have difficulty conducting a civilized conversation with them."

They turned to walk back toward Belladonna when suddenly

the ice behind them began to tremble and crack. With a
splintering roar the ice broke and through it came the heads of
the killer whales, savage teeth gleaming in their open mouths.

"Wow!" yelled Lancelot. "The silly fools are hunting us. Run
for it, children, run, run."

They rushed off across the ice with the killer whales, crashing
behind them in hot pursuit.

"What was it you said about them being nice, friendly chaps?"
asked Conrad, as he and Ivan each took one of Lancelot's arms to
hurry him along.

Suddenly there was a series of booming crashes and Lancelot
and the children found themselves marooned on a large slab of
ice. In a circle around them was a ring of menacing killer whales.
Lancelot and the children were completely cut off.

"What are we going to do?" asked Emma, terrified by the glittering white teeth that surrounded them.

"All together now," said Lancelot. "WE ARE FRIENDS!"

They shouted as loudly as they could. All the killer whales, heads out of the water, listened politely.

"My dear sir, why didn't you say so before?" inquired the largest whale, whose head was uncomfortably close to them. "We do beg your pardon. We thought you were seals."

"No harm done," said Lancelot, very relieved, "but I'd be glad if you'd shove this iceberg a bit closer to the shore, so that we can get off. We're frightened of falling into the water."

"With the greatest of pleasure," said Killer Whale, and with his huge, shining snout he pushed the raft of ice to the shore.

They all felt much safer once they were on a firm surface once more.

"Thank you. I wonder if you can direct us to a polar bear?" Lancelot asked the large killer whale.

"Yes," said Killer Whale, musingly. "I think I can oblige you. There's a den over there. But be careful how you treat her. She has only just woken up from her winter hibernation."

"They can be funny mammals, polar bears," agreed Lancelot.

"Yes," smiled Killer Whale, "not even-tempered like us."

With that they slid out of sight beneath the water.

"Phew. That was close," muttered Lancelot, relieved. "Now let's get along to that polar bear's den they pointed out."

They set off cautiously toward a great mound of snow. When they were nearly there, Lancelot pointed and whispered, "That's the den, but we won't go too close until we see what sort of mood she's in."

"Look! I can see steam rising out of a tiny hole in the snow," said Emma excitedly.

They watched the den nervously for several minutes. Then there was a flurry of snow and the head of a polar bear emerged. She sniffed the air with her long black nose, then eased her huge body out of the den. She growled, and two cubs followed her out onto the ice. They looked around with big, dark eyes.

"Why, the mother's coat is almost yellow," whispered Conrad, in surprise, "but the babies are as white as the snow."

"Help!" yelled Lancelot suddenly. The snow was giving way under him and he started to slide toward the bears.

The polar bear looked up angrily as a huge wad of snow thudded down in front of her. Conrad reached out and managed to grab Lancelot's sleeve.

"Friend," shouted Lancelot quickly. "Sorry. Accident. Slipped."

Then the snow gave way completely and he fell off right in front of the polar bear. The children watched in horror, certain that the irritated animal would eat Lancelot.

Polar Bear sniffed at him with her black nose.

"You smell like Perceval," she said, "though you seem to have put on a lot of weight. I thought you'd gone south to visit the buffaloes."

"I'm his brother," muttered Lancelot, not knowing whether to be angry or frightened. "We've come to the Arctic to find him."

"Well, you've missed him. He left here a year ago. Do stop quivering," Polar Bear grunted. "I won't eat you. Any friend of Perceval is a friend of mine."

Lancelot got to his feet. He tried to look dignified.

"I was *not* quivering," he insisted. "I was shivering with cold."

It was certainly true that they were all feeling a bit chilly. Lancelot's nose was very blue and he absentmindedly rubbed it with snow to stop it from getting frostbite.

"What adorable babies you have," said Emma, truthfully, but at the same time hoping it would put Polar Bear in a better mood.

"Huh!" snorted Polar Bear. "You wouldn't think that if you had to spend all winter in a small den with them kicking you in the stomach. Just as you drift off to sleep, they wriggle and squirm. When they grow older it's: 'Mom, can we go out for a walk?' and 'Mom can we have a drink?' It's enough to make you give up hibernation, I can tell you."

"Would you mind if we looked inside your den?" asked Conrad.

"Not at all," said the bear, hospitably.

One by one the children crawled down the ice tunnel to a small, cold, circular room. Here the mother had hibernated and the young had been born. A strange greenish light filtered through the ice and snow. Emma found a lovely white tuft of baby fur and put it carefully in her pocket. Later, she promised herself, she would stick it in the diary.

When they emerged from the ice tunnel, they found Polar Bear impatiently waiting for them.

"Well," said Polar Bear, "I must be off. I haven't had breakfast yet and I need to keep up my strength with these two to look after."

She slouched off across the ice, followed by her babies, wrestling and pummeling each other as they went. The children waved good-bye, then turned toward Belladonna.

"Why don't polar bears slip on the ice?" asked Emma.

"Because the soles of their paws are covered with fur," explained Lancelot, "and that stops them from slipping. Well, come on now, we must head south to the buffaloes. We'll visit the musk-oxen on the way. We can pick up some more of their fur."

As they flew southward, the snow and ice started to disappear. Soon they were floating over the greeny-yellow tundra. They caught sight of a herd of reindeer grazing, and Lancelot took Belladonna down low to try to get news of the musk-oxen.

The ground looked like a thick carpet of moss. It was studded with thousands of tiny flowers which were all the colors of the rainbow. Even the trees were miniature, few growing above knee height.

As they neared the reindeer, the children were surprised to see that they were every shade of brown and yellow, from chocolate to butter. The nearest reindeer was a huge cocoa-colored male whose massive antlers were like a tree.

"Ahoy, there," shouted Lancelot through his megaphone. "Have you seen any musk-oxen?"

The reindeer's voice floated up faintly from below.

"There are some about six miles to the south. But watch out for the wolves. They're out in force at the moment and causing a lot of trouble."

"Wolves!" snorted Lancelot. "I'm not afraid of wolves."

They continued southward. A few minutes later, Lancelot

spied a herd of about twenty musk-oxen. They were grazing on a raised hillock in the otherwise flat tundra.

"There they are, my friends, the musk-oxen," he said, affectionately. "Looking fat and healthy and with six new babies, if I'm not mistaken," he added.

Suddenly he stiffened, glaring through the telescope.

"Look," he cried, agitated. "Wolves! Creeping up on the herd. We've got to do something quickly."

Through the telescope, the children could see a large pack of wolves slinking closer and closer to the musk-oxen, who were grazing quietly oblivious to the imminent danger.

Lancelot rushed into the control room and tried to increase speed. But Belladonna was already going full steam ahead. Her silken ropes were twanging in the rushing air and the veranda was tilting dangerously over to one side.

"We're too far away," cried Emma, despairingly.

Just at that moment the wolves appeared over the rim of the plateau, running fast. The musk-oxen, after a moment's horror and confusion, formed a circle, facing outward, presenting a bristling

wall of horns to their enemies. All the babies were safely in the middle of this fortress. The wolves started to circle them, getting closer with each step.

"We must do something," said Emma. "Haven't you got a gun?"

"No, I don't carry a gun," said Lancelot. "It frightens the animals you know, all that banging. Stop a minute . . . banging, that's it, I've got the very thing!"

He rushed off and soon returned carrying a huge box.

"Fireworks," he panted. "Got them in case we had a celebration. These should do the trick. The noise will frighten off the wolves without hurting them."

Belladonna flew low until she was over the circling wolves.

"Now," said Lancelot, lighting a match. "Fire!"

In next to no time the flashing, multicolored rockets burst into the sky, roman candles spouted flames and sparks, pinwheels whirled to and fro and firecrackers went off with deafening reports. The wolves, taken by surprise, had no idea how to cope with this unknown type of attack. Yelping and howling with fear, they streaked away as fast as they could.

Lancelot and the children cheered wildly and they could hear the musk-oxen mooing their appreciation. Lancelot brought Belladonna down to rest and they rushed out to be greeted by a great shaggy and very relieved musk-ox.

"My dear sir," said Musk-Ox, snorting out a great cloud of frosty air, "never have I seen wolves put to flight like that. Quite remarkable. What are those noisy things called?"

"Fireworks," said Lancelot. "Most useful, aren't they?"

"Yes indeed and we're very grateful to you. Now, what are you here for? More of our wool? You're most welcome to it."

"That's very kind," said Lancelot. "We will gather some wool, thank you. It's just the thing to insulate our balloon against the cold. But I really intended this to be a friendly visit. I wanted my niece and nephews to meet you."

"How nice of you to come all this way," boomed Musk-Ox to the children. "Any friend of Lancelot's is always welcome. Now, come and meet my family."

"Don't be too long, then," said Lancelot. "We have to fly on south to look for my brother," he explained to Musk-Ox, "so this will have to be a short visit."

"Oh, please," chorused the children. "Please, Lancelot, let us go and meet the rest of the musk-oxen."

"Off you go, then," said Lancelot kindly. "Off you go."

The children had a wonderful time with the musk-oxen. They

galloped about the tundra on the backs of the bigger ones. They combed one huge musk-ox, collecting its fine underfur in sacks. They found the fur was as soft as dandelion puffs. Emma decided that she would use some of it to knit sweaters for all the family when she got home.

Finally, the children found themselves yawning their heads off. They headed back to where Lancelot was stomping up and down to keep himself warm.

"I wonder why we're so tired," said Emma.

"It's because it's summer and the sun shines all the time here," said Lancelot. "There's no night at this time and we've been up for fourteen hours."

"I bet we sleep well tonight," said the twins.

"So do I," said Emma.

Reluctantly they parted from their furry friends the musk-oxen and climbed aboard Belladonna. The children collapsed into bed and slept soundly as the balloon continued her journey south.

CHAPTER SIX

OFF THE BEATEN TRACK

Several mornings later, Belladonna was anchored by the shores of a beautiful lake in North America. The blue water was so calm that the tall pine trees were reflected perfectly. The twins amused themselves by standing on their heads and looking at their reflections.

Everything seemed perfect, but Emma was very worried. Lancelot was missing again. When they had got up for breakfast he had not been there, though he must have remembered how worried they had been when he disappeared in Australia, because this time he had left a letter. It read: *Got up early to look for a moose. Will follow the lake shore to the east. Back for breakfast—three eggs sunny side up please. Love, Lancelot.*

The only problem was that it was now lunchtime and there was no sign of him. Something must have gone very wrong.

"We must launch a rescue party," Emma announced to the twins. "You pack a backpack and I'll write a note to leave here, telling him where we've gone, just in case he returns."

Conrad and Ivan put the survival gear into the backpack. This time, instead of salt tablets, they put in a flask of hot coffee.

"That way is east," announced Ivan, looking at the compass on his knife. "Come on, there's no time to lose."

They hiked along the edge of the lake, stopping every few minutes to shout Lancelot's name. They listened carefully for a reply, but heard nothing except the echoes of their own voices.

"Where can he be?" Emma was in despair and close to tears.

"Moose spend most of their time grazing in lakes and rivers," reasoned Conrad, "so we'll find him if we keep on as we are."

"I just hope he isn't hurt," sniffed Emma, wiping her eyes.

"Nothing could hurt Lancelot," said Conrad.

"Nothing would dare," added Ivan, and Emma gave a pale smile.

A few minutes later, Ivan stopped suddenly.

"Quiet!" he said. "I thought I heard something."

They strained their ears but could hear nothing.

"Let's all shout together," suggested Emma.

"LANCELOT! LANCELOT!" they bellowed, then paused, absolutely still. A faint cry came from somewhere ahead.

"Help, help, over here!"

They ran forward. Lancelot was lying under a huge tree, pinned down by its branches.

"Thank goodness you've come," gasped Lancelot. "I thought I was going to be here all day. I tried to climb that slope and pulled on the branches of this tree to help me up. The roots must have been loose and the stupid thing fell on top of me."

"Are you hurt?" asked Emma.

"No, I'm fine, just stuck," replied Lancelot. The children tugged at the tree but couldn't manage to shift it at all.

"Whatever can we do?"

asked Ivan.

Lancelot thought for a moment, then said, "There's a beaver lodge a little farther around the lake. I found it earlier. Run and bring a beaver to help me."

The twins went off and soon came upon a great, fat, brown beaver, busily gnawing away at a small pine tree.

"Excuse me," said Ivan, "we're in trouble and need your help."

"I'm very busy at the moment," replied Beaver, a feverish glint in his eye. "Repair work on the dam."

"Please," begged Conrad. "Our uncle is trapped under a tree and we need your help to get him out."

"Ah, an emergency. That's different," Beaver replied. "Just lead the way and we'll have him out in a flash."

A few minutes later Beaver was looking at Lancelot's tree.

"Now let me see. If I just cut here and here," he mused, marking the bark with his great chisel-shaped teeth, "that should do the trick. I'll have him out in fifteen minutes."

"But the trunk's a foot and a half thick," gasped Ivan.

Beaver set to work. Chips of wood flew in all directions. In a very short time there was a creaking crash and part of the tree slid down the slope. Lancelot was free and right as rain.

"Now," Beaver announced, after they had thanked him, "I really must get on. But do come and meet my family and see our home."

The beaver dam was a huge tangle of branches. It was six-and-a-half feet high and twenty feet thick. Beaver started his repair work straightaway.

"Why do you think beavers build dams?" asked Lancelot.

"To stop the flow of the stream and create a pond for the beavers to live in?" suggested Ivan.

"Yes, of course!" cried Emma. "And the dam protects their home from other animals."

"Well done," said Lancelot, pointing downstream to where the dam had reduced the water to a trickle. Behind the dam lay a large area of placid water. The children could see what looked like half of a giant football made from twigs and mud sticking up in the middle of the pond.

"That's their home," he explained. "It's called a lodge. They live and store food there. They eat bark."

"The pond must help the beavers too," said Emma, starting to sketch the lodge. "They can keep food safe from animals which don't swim as well as they do. But how do they get in and out of the lodge?"

"There must be an underwater entrance," guessed Ivan.

Beaver had dragged several new logs onto the dam and the trickle of water over the top had stopped. He swam over.

"Water's stopped," he grunted, "so I can take a rest."

"Tell me," said Emma. "What do you do when you use up all the trees nearby? What happens to your dam and your food supply?"

"We build canals," explained Beaver, surprised that Emma did not know this, "and float trees down to the pond."

At that moment, a baby beaver slapped his flat tail on the surface of the water, making a sound like a gunshot.

"Oh no! That's the alarm call. He must have seen that moose after the water lilies. It wallows about under the water pulling up lily roots and disturbing all the mud so we can't see a thing," complained Beaver crossly.

"We'll go up and see what's happening," said Lancelot.

They said good-bye to the beavers and walked around the edge of the pond. Soon, they came to a spot where the pond widened out into what was really a small lake, its surface starred with the most beautiful white and yellow water lilies.

A little way from the shore there was a great disturbance taking place in the water, as if some monstrous fish was searching for food beneath the surface. Suddenly the muddy waters of the lake foamed and boiled. Like a huge sea monster, the head of a bull moose, his antlers covered with a tangle of water lilies, emerged from the lake.

"Hah," snorted Moose, staring at them as he blew water out of his nostrils and making his huge nose wobble from side to side. "Good day. Who might you all be?"

"Travelers," said Lancelot in a friendly tone. "We've just been to see the beavers. They are upset about all the mud you're making. Couldn't you go somewhere else?"

"But this is the best spot I've ever found for water lilies," protested Moose. "I come here once a year to feed on them. I know the beavers make a fuss about the mud, but they don't realize that the lily roots are essential to my well-being."

"You mean like a medicine, or vitamins?" asked Emma.

"Exactly," replied Moose. "The lily roots improve my muscles and make my antlers bigger."

"I wouldn't have thought you needed bigger antlers," said Conrad in amazement.

"Oh yes," said Moose. "I need them for fighting my rivals in the mating season, and for driving off wolves. They are one of the most important parts of my body, perhaps *the* most important."

"Talking of bodies," said Conrad rather flippantly, "what's yours like? All we can see is your head!"

"So you want to see what I look like?" said Moose. "Well, so you shall."

With much heaving and splashing, Moose got to his feet. He was enormous, almost six-and-a-half feet high!

"What do you eat besides water lilies?" asked Ivan, raising his voice a little, for Moose now seemed so tall that Ivan thought he might have difficulty in hearing.

"Oh, leaves, fresh bark, moss, mushrooms and other fungi," said Moose, shaking his antlers so that bouquets of water lilies fell off.

"I must say, I do admire your antlers," said Emma, who couldn't stop staring at them. "If only we could take one home with us."

"You want one of my antlers?" asked Moose. "That's no problem. We moose, like other deer, shed our antlers every year and grow new ones. Behind that big tree over there is one of my last year's antlers. You can have that if you like."

Greatly excited, the children ran off to the tree which Moose had indicated. Behind it they found an antler as big as half a door. It took all three of them to carry it.

"Well, we must be off to find the buffaloes," said Lancelot, after he'd taken a photograph of Moose and of the children struggling to carry the antler. "Thank you for the antler."

"Not at all," said Moose, politely. "It's of no use to *me* anymore, it will only get chewed up by porcupines."

Then Moose turned away and continued munching.

Two days later, they were floating serenely over a vast prairie of undulating grass. As they dropped lower, they saw that there were hundreds of patches of bare earth dotted with what looked like miniature volcanoes.

"What on earth are those?" Emma asked Lancelot curiously.

"They're prairie dog towns," he replied. "Nice little fellows, prairie dogs. We'll drop in and have a word with them."

But when they landed and started to walk among the hillocks, there was not a single prairie dog to be seen anywhere.

"How strange," said Emma. "Where do you think they've gone?"

"Perhaps it's a deserted town," suggested Conrad. "You know, like one of those ghost towns in the Wild West."

"Oh, it's not deserted," said Lancelot. "I expect they saw us coming and hid. They probably thought Belladonna was a giant hawk. They're terrified of hawks, so I expect they're cowering in their burrows for safety."

They crouched down by a burrow.

"Ahoy, there, you prairie dogs," Lancelot shouted. "Come out and have a chat with us. We're quite harmless and friendly. We just want to say hello."

There was a great deal of scuffling and squeaking in the depths of the burrow. Then he heard a shrill voice.

"Who are you and what do you want?" it asked.

"We're just friendly travelers who want to have a word with you," shouted Lancelot. "Come out, don't be afraid."

"Any hawks about?" asked the voice suspiciously.

"No, you're quite safe," chorused the children.

"Well, I might just pop out for a moment," said the voice. "No tricks, though. I've got very sharp teeth and a terrible temper when I'm roused."

There was more scuffling and scraping, then suddenly a prairie dog popped out of his hole.

"Well," he said, sitting on his hind legs, "you're a curious-looking bunch, though I must say you look friendly enough."

"What an enormous town you have here," said Ivan, watching in amazement as hundreds of other prairie dogs began to emerge.

"Yes, it's quite big," Prairie Dog agreed. "There are about a thousand of us, living in twenty-five coteries or groups."

"Why are you so afraid of hawks?" asked Conrad.

"Well now, 'afraid' is perhaps the wrong word," said Prairie Dog, a trifle huffily. "We're not afraid exactly, we just don't like them. We can get away easily enough from other enemies like coyotes and rattlesnakes, but hawks have a nasty habit of zooming down on us suddenly when we least expect it. We have to keep alert the whole time.''

They were discussing the evil habits of hawks when Prairie Dog suddenly stiffened and glared at another prairie dog who was sauntering past.

''Excuse me a moment,'' said Prairie Dog. ''I must go and straighten this fellow out.''

He lollopped across the mounds and caught up with his quarry, who turned to face him.

''Now look here,'' he said. ''You'd better push off. This is not your territory. You know you don't belong here.''

The other prairie dog merely stood up on his hind legs and chattered his teeth.

''Oh, so that's what you want,'' said Prairie Dog, his temper rising. Chattering his own teeth most ferociously in reply, he suddenly dived at his opponent. In a moment the two animals became a rolling ball of fur, punching, biting and scratching each other. They whirled around and around in a cloud of dust while all the other prairie dogs gathered to watch.

''Go on!'' they squeaked. ''Bite his nose off, blacken his eyes,

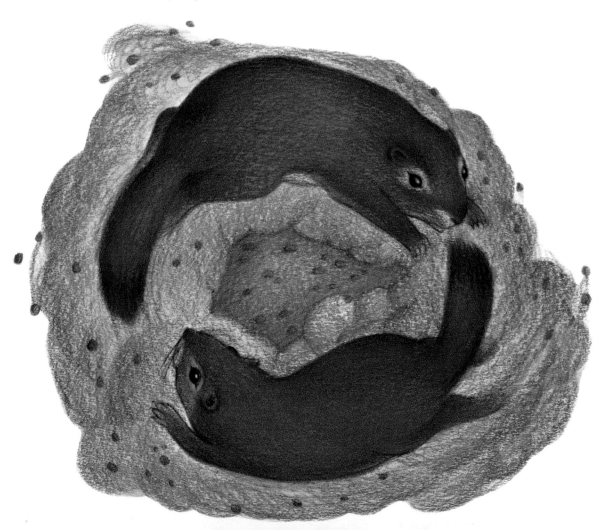

skin his tail, zonk him on the
head, stamp on his paws!"

Before any of the suggestions
could be put into effect, the
strange prairie dog decided he'd had
enough and broke away. He ran off at
full speed and disappeared over the
horizon. The victorious prairie dog
came back, bloodstained but triumphant.

"That'll teach him," he said, chuckling.
"He won't be around here for a while, I can tell
you. I really mashed him."

"Why did you fight him?" asked Ivan.
"He seemed quite harmless."

"Harmless indeed," squeaked Prairie Dog. "He was an
intruder, just trying it on. Animals from other coteries will often
take a fancy to our town. If they can get away with it, they move
in and set up home in half our burrows. No, he was a spy and it's
a good thing I spotted him."

"I think it was clever of you to spot him," said Emma, "and
very brave of you to tackle him like that."

Just then Conrad noticed a large cloud of dust on the far
distant edges of the prairie dog town.

"What's that?" he asked.

"Buffaloes," replied Prairie Dog, "blast their horns and hides.
They're rolling on our homes. They like the dust, you see. It
cleans their skin and hair. But can you imagine what it's like to
have a great big animal like a buffalo rolling about on top of your
home? It's like having an earthquake twice a day. Tunnels fall in,
there are avalanches of soil in all the rooms, you have to rescue
your children before they suffocate. It's a real nightmare." He
sighed.

At that moment a large hawk came into sight, flying low and
purposefully toward the town.

Immediately, all the prairie dogs started barking, making a
terrific noise which suddenly ceased as they all dived down their
holes. There was not a single one left in sight.

"Come on," said Lancelot. "They won't be out again for a
while. Let's go and talk to those buffaloes."

It took them almost an hour to reach the buffalo herd. The swirling dust made it hard for them to see where they were going. It stung their eyes and made breathing difficult.

"It's almost like that terrible desert sandstorm," said Emma, coughing as the dust flew into her mouth.

But gradually the dust settled, and they could see the herd of buffaloes in the distance. It looked like a huge brown woolly rug thrown down onto the green prairie. As they drew nearer, the children could hear all around them the steady munching sound of hundreds of buffaloes grazing. The leader was a massive animal covered with thick, curly hair. He had an imposing beard that put even Lancelot's to shame.

"Well, now," he said in a deep, sleepy voice. "And what may you want?"

"We're looking for our Great-Uncle Perceval," explained Conrad. "He's lost."

"We've followed him all the way from Africa. First to Australia and then to the North Pole," added Emma.

"Polar Bear told us that he had come south to study the buffaloes. Have you seen him?" asked Lancelot.

"Yes, indeed," answered Buffalo. "He was here for about a week talking to us. But I'm afraid he left about nine months ago.

He said he was going to the Amazon to do some research into
howler monkeys."

"Oh, no!" groaned Lancelot. "We'll never find him at this rate."

"What was he doing here?" asked Ivan.

"He was writing a history of the buffaloes and wanted to know
what really happened to us," replied Buffalo.

"Will you tell us too?" asked Emma, getting out the diary.

"I will, but I must warn you that it is a very sad story," replied
Buffalo. "Though it does have a happy ending."

The children and Lancelot sat down to listen.

"Once," began Buffalo, "the prairies were just a huge moving
carpet of buffaloes. There were over ten million of us. Some
herds were so large they would take two days to pass a single
point. As we moved about we wore away roads with our hooves,
roads that were later used by humans. But now, there are only
five thousand buffaloes left."

Tears appeared in his great brown eyes and trickled down his
cheeks into his beard. Emma took out her handkerchief and
wiped Buffalo's face.

"Only five thousand!" gasped Conrad. "How did that happen?"

Buffalo looked at them, hesitated, then replied, "In a word,
humans. Our story is an awful warning about what humans can do."

"In the beginning, you see, we were hunted by the Indians, but there weren't too many of them, so it didn't matter so much. At least we were important to them. Our hides provided them with clothes and tents. They ate our flesh and even made things like needles out of our bones. Not a single bit of us was wasted.

"It wasn't so bad being killed as long as we felt we were *useful*, but when the white humans arrived things changed. They started to build huge railroads from one side of America to the other. They brought guns with them. At least with the Indians' bows and arrows we had some chance to escape, but we couldn't escape the guns.

"When the trains started, the white humans organized so-called hunting parties. People simply sat in the carriages and shot the buffaloes out of the window. But what was so awful was that they didn't even bother to take the bodies for food or skins. They simply left them there to rot."

Buffalo gave a great sob and another tear ran down his cheek. Emma took out her handkerchief again.

"Disgusting, quite disgusting," she said, angrily.

"I read somewhere that the smell of rotting meat was so great, they had to keep the carriage windows closed," said Lancelot. "It was a revolting thing to do."

"Finally," said Buffalo, "there were only a hundred and fifty of us left. Fortunately, there were some humans who realized that unless something was done we would vanish from the earth all together. They created a special reserve for us and protected us. So slowly our numbers are increasing, but it was touch and go whether we survived or not."

"It's a terrible story," said Ivan.

"Makes your blood run cold," said Conrad.

"I don't wonder it upsets you, you poor thing," said Emma.

"I'm so sorry we made you cry."

"I'm just a sentimental old fool," said Buffalo.

"You're not!" said Emma, indignantly, wiping his eyes again. "If it had been my family and my ancestors, I would have cried buckets."

"Well, things are better now," said Buffalo. "We are protected and no one can hunt us anymore."

Buffalo raised his head and looked proudly around him.

"When we stampede, the prairie still trembles to the thunder of our hooves," he snorted. Then he shook his head and pawed the ground, throwing up a cloud of dust.

"Would you mind if I cut off a tiny curl from your beard to remind us of this meeting?" asked Emma, producing a pair of scissors from her pocket.

"Not at all," said Buffalo. "Help yourself."

So Emma cut a great, brown, soft ringlet from his beard and pressed it between the pages of the diary.

"We must be moving on," said Lancelot to Buffalo. "We have a long journey ahead of us across Mexico and down to South America in search of this rascally brother of mine."

He turned to the children. "Say good-bye to the buffaloes and we'll get back to Belladonna."

So they said their farewells and left the herd of buffaloes grazing placidly.

"What a very sad story," said Conrad as they walked back to Belladonna.

"Humans have made lots of mistakes in the past," agreed Lancelot, "but many people are now working to improve things for animals."

"We've learned a lot on this journey," said Conrad. "We must make sure we use that knowledge to help wildlife when we get home."

"Of course we will," the others agreed.

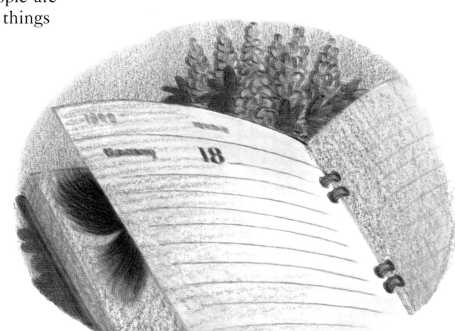

CHAPTER SEVEN

DIVERSIONS AND DANGERS

It was Ivan who first spotted the danger, for he was on the veranda watching the passing countryside, while the others were below. Lancelot was baking some bread, Conrad was feeding the spiders and Emma was working on the buffalo section of the diary. They all heard Ivan's terrified shout.

"Lancelot! Lancelot! Come quickly," he yelled. "There's a huge sort of . . . thing . . . that's going to bump into us!"

They all rushed up onto the veranda and a terrible and menacing sight met their eyes. About a half mile away, there was a huge, black column of earth. It was six hundred to a thousand feet high and was advancing toward them with a swirling, undulating motion like a snake. They could see, as it twisted and writhed its way toward them, that it was ripping up trees and bushes and tearing the roofs off barns and houses, sucking them up into its whirling column of mud.

"Great heavens!" exclaimed Lancelot.
"It's a twister. That's what they call a tornado
hereabouts. If that hits us we've really had it."

So saying, he rushed into the control room and put
Belladonna into reverse at full speed. Then there was
nothing they could do but stand on the veranda and watch.
With horror-stricken eyes they saw the swirling menace getting
closer and closer. Then they heard the noise it was making. It
was a whooshing, windy sort of noise, together with a snarly,
grating, scrunching sort of noise, like someone snoring, hissing,
gargling and brushing his teeth all at the same time. It was a
sound so horrific that their blood ran cold.

"Oh, Lancelot," said Emma, in a tremulous voice, for she was
very frightened indeed. "Are we really going to be hit?"

"I don't know, I just don't know," said Lancelot. "I'm afraid it
looks like it. There's nothing we can do except pray for a miracle
to happen."

And then, as if in answer to Lancelot's prayer, a miracle *did*
happen. The tornado was now about fifty feet away from
Belladonna. The twisting column of earth was creating such a
wind that it actually blew Belladonna out of its way. It snarled
and hissed as it brushed past them, showering the veranda with

pebbles, earth, branches, leaves, dead fish, live frogs, one water tortoise and two birds' nests with the eggs still in them.

The wind was so fierce that the veranda rocked violently and they all fell in a tangled heap together. Ivan accidentally kicked Conrad in the face, giving him a black eye. Emma was thrown violently on top of Lancelot's large tummy, winding him so he lay, gasping for breath like a huge, hairy fish. But as they lay, the tornado went past them, whistling and twisting on its destructive way.

"Oh, oh," moaned Lancelot loudly, "my poor head and my poor tummy. I'm sure I shall die. Indeed, I'm not at all sure I'm not dead already."

He went on and on like this and nothing would pacify him until Emma put a hot water bottle on his stomach.

The children set about cleaning up the mess. They swept the veranda, keeping some of the twigs, leaves and stones and the two birds' nests as souvenirs. They fed the dead fish to the electric eels, who immediately, in gratitude, started to give out more volts of electricity. They flew low over a lake to return the grateful water tortoise and the frogs to their watery homes.

The next morning, Emma was the first up and, having put the kettle on, she made her way out onto the veranda.

Here, an incredible sight met her astonished eyes. "Good gracious!" she gasped. "Come and look at this."

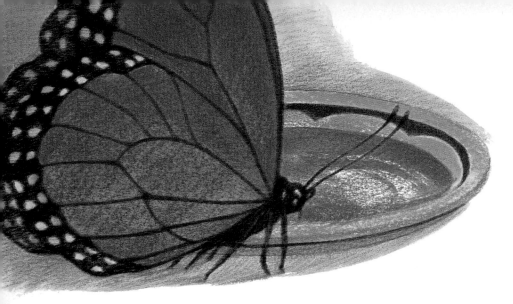

"Good heavens!" Lancelot exclaimed, coming out onto the veranda. "Monarch butterflies off on their migration, I'll bet."

The whole veranda, the wheelhouse and the silken ropes that attached the bamboo house to the balloon were covered with thousands upon thousands of huge butterflies. They were all restlessly moving their orange, red and black wings with a gentle, rustling sound.

"Yes, off to Mexico for the winter," said a butterfly, perching on Lancelot's nose. "Are you going in our direction?"

"Not if you keep tickling my nose," said Lancelot, firmly.

"Sorry," said the butterfly and flew onto Emma's head.

"Where have you come from?" asked Emma.

"Canada," replied Butterfly.

"My goodness, that's a long haul," exclaimed Lancelot. "You'll be glad of a rest. Whereabouts in Mexico do you want to go?"

"There's a special valley we go to," said Butterfly dreamily. "It's so beautiful, with lovely pine trees."

"Beautiful, beautiful, beautiful," chanted all the monarchs.

"We hang onto the trunks of the trees and sleep," said Butterfly. "Then when the sun comes out, we drink at a beautiful little river."

"Beautiful, beautiful, beautiful," sang all the insects, opening and closing their wings in a moving tapestry of color.

"And then we go to sleep again," said Butterfly, "until the winter is over and summer is back with us. That's when we fly back to Canada."

"Well, if you know the way to this valley, we'll take you there on our way to the Amazon," said Lancelot.

"Thank you, thank you," said all the monarchs in their soft, tremulous, silvery voices.

"Isn't the flight from Canada to Mexico terribly long and dangerous?" asked Emma. "Why do you do it?"

"Don't ask me," said Butterfly, sipping delicately at the saucer of honey Emma had provided. "We copy our parents."

"It must be very curious being a butterfly," said Emma.

"No more so than being human," Butterfly pointed out. "You pass through different stages too, just like we do."

"What do you mean?" she asked.

"Well," said Butterfly. "The first stage with us is a cozy, green egg. All the sights and sounds of the world are dimmed. You just eat the delicious yolk in the egg and grow bigger. When, eventually, you decide it's time to gnaw your way out of the shell, the scents almost suffocate you. The colors are blinding and the noise is deafening."

"I suppose that is how a human baby feels," said Emma. "Safe inside his or her mother one minute, then out in a new world of colors, scents and noise the next. It must be very frightening."

"Yes," said Butterfly, taking another sip of honey. "But you soon get used to it. And you eat and grow until, one day, you get a curious feeling. As though somehow you had become dissatisfied with your skin and wanted to get out of it."

"So you find yourself a suitable spot and hang yourself up by your tail," he continued. "Then you feel yourself changing and turning into something else. Off comes your skin and you're a handsome chrysalis. It's really rather like being in a different-shaped egg again. Slowly you feel yourself change, until one day, you know it's time to hatch. You give a few mighty wriggles, the chrysalis splits along the back and out you come, changed from a caterpillar into a butterfly. Of course, inside the chrysalis, you've had your wings all folded up, like a . . . like a . . ." Butterfly hesitated.

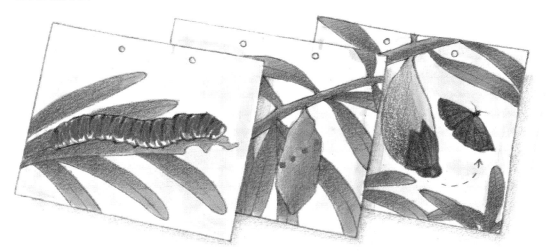

"Like a concertina," suggested Conrad.

"Yes," agreed Butterfly. "Your wings are very soft and crumpled, so you have to pump blood into the veins to expand them and then dry them in the sun until they're hard. Then comes the most exciting moment of all—your first flight, dancing in the breeze to find your first delicious sip of nectar."

"It sounds wonderful," said Emma.

"It is, it is," said Butterfly, dreamily. "You find a wife, she lays eggs and the whole thing starts over again. Then you're ready for your rest in Mexico. Beautiful."

"I say, Butterfly," shouted Lancelot. "I think we must be getting quite close to your valley."

The children saw that Belladonna was floating through great clouds of butterflies all heading in the same direction. The air was filled with silvery voices calling greetings to each other, exchanging news and gossip.

Insects from Canada mingled with insects from different parts of the United States. Gradually, Belladonna dropped through the clouds of monarchs and finally landed in a valley. It was just as Butterfly had described, with a forest of pine trees on the sides and a stream running through the center.

They walked among the trees and marveled at what they saw.

Every branch and every tree trunk was covered with unimaginable numbers of butterflies, some asleep, others slowly opening and closing their wings and chattering together. Others still were flying in glittering procession to drink at the little stream.

Emma and the twins felt they were in a butterfly kingdom, for everywhere they looked there were monarchs. A steady, swirling stream was still flying in from the north. These millions of wings made a soft, swishing sound like somebody whirling a piece of silk, and a million silver voices sounded like sleigh bells on a winter's night. The whole thing was so beautiful that they were reluctant to drag themselves away.

Finally, they returned to Belladonna where they ate a lovely Mexican meal prepared by Lancelot. It contained black beans, sweet green peppers, chicken, chick-peas and tomatoes. Then they tumbled into bed and were soon fast asleep.

The children would never forget their first sight of the mighty Amazon a few days later. They knew they were approaching it long before land was in sight, because they saw a huge, coiling, brown streak lying in the blue sea. Lancelot explained that this was a band of fresh water and mud brought down by the great river and spewed out into the ocean.

As they were floating along, Emma spotted a huge tree trunk in the water. On it was coiled an enormous boa constrictor, the biggest snake she had ever seen in her life.

"He's marooned, poor thing," said Lancelot, "Come on, we'll have to save him."

They took Belladonna down low and dropped a silken ladder over the side. With much hissing and wriggling, the snake managed to weave his way through the rungs of the ladder. Lancelot and Ivan hauled the huge serpent onto the veranda.

"This is a novel way of playing snakes and ladders," chuckled Lancelot, trying to reassure Conrad, who was feeling a bit nervous, remembering his adventure with the spitting cobra.

"How do you feel, old chap?" he asked.

"Very much better now, thank you," replied Boa, in a hissing voice. "I am most grateful to you for rescuing me."

"How did you get into such difficulties?" asked Emma.

"A storm blew my tree into the water and I was marooned," explained Boa. "As I was trying to shed my skin at the time, I was blind because of the scales over my eyes. So I just clung on for dear life. Saltwater kept getting up my nose but worst of all, I couldn't change my skin. So if it's convenient to you and you don't mind, I'd rather like to shed it now."

"By all means," said Lancelot. "Go ahead, don't mind us."

"You're very kind," said Boa Constrictor. "Here we go."

They watched him, fascinated, as he writhed around the veranda. In a very short time he had wriggled out of his skin completely, leaving it lying on the deck, like a sort of shadow of himself.

"Ah, that's better," he said, coiling up comfortably.

"It's inside out, like someone taking off a sock," said Ivan taking a closer look.

"It's more transparent than tracing paper," added Conrad, "and you can see every scale, look, even the ones covering the eyes."

"It's lovely," said Emma. "It's like a cross between parchment and lace. I'd love to have a skin like that."

"What, my old skin?" asked the Boa in surprise. "Would you like it?"

"Yes, please," replied Emma. "It's beautiful, thanks so much."

As Belladonna rose once again into the sky, Boa went to sleep, coiled and still, while his skin dried in the sun.

"He has no eyelids, just a scale over each eye," whispered Ivan, as they all stood watching him.

"He must sleep with his eyes open," Emma said in astonishment.

They all tiptoed away and left Boa Constrictor to his rest.

When Boa woke up, Lancelot cooked a splendid South American dish called Pochero. It was rather like an Irish stew with everything in it.

Boa joined them for lunch but he only ate a dozen or so raw eggs instead, which he pronounced to be delicious. Afterward they all lay around looking at the river below, hot from the sun, feeling very full and relaxed. Emma rested her head on Boa's coils. They were as comfy as a cushion.

In the tops of the towering trees that lined the riverbank they could see hummingbirds flitting from flower to flower. They glinted and gleamed in the sun. Toucans with great yellow beaks, like the noses clowns wear in the circus, flapped from tree to tree feeding on the fruits.

"Tell me," Emma asked Boa, "there's something I've always wanted to know. How do snakes manage to move along?"

"Why, we walk on our ribs, of course," said Boa in astonishment. "I thought everyone knew that. If you lie still, I'll crawl over you so you can see how it's done."

So Emma lay flat on her back and Boa slowly drew himself across her body. She could feel all his ribs moving under his skin like little legs. It was a most curious experience, rather like feeling a giant caterpillar walking over you.

"You must be awfully strong," said Conrad, who had been watching Boa with interest.

"Awfully," agreed Boa. "My body is one huge muscle, really."

"Can you show us how strong you are?" asked Ivan.

"Well, I can give you a bit of a squeeze if you like," said Boa. "If you all get together, that is."

So the children and Lancelot all stood back to back. Boa coiled around them like a huge necklace and began to squeeze. In a very short time they were gasping for breath and pleading for mercy.

"Now that's enough of that," panted Lancelot, rubbing his bruised ribs. "I'm going to the flight deck. You can all stay here and enjoy the view."

Soon Lancelot brought Belladonna lower, following the line of the huge river as it wound its way, coffee-colored and glinting through the thick, magnificent rain forest. The forest was like an undulating sea of leaves, starred here and there with masses of colored flowers and fruits. The air was hot and damp, so it felt like being in a greenhouse.

Lancelot suddenly peered out from the flight deck. "Is there anywhere special you want to go?" he asked Boa.

"No, anywhere will do," replied the snake.

"Well, I'm going to land my electric eels and spiders at the next bend in the river," said Lancelot. "They've had a tough

journey. We were a bit knocked about by a tornado, you
see," he explained, "so I thought I ought to take on a new
crew. Will the next bend in the river suit you?"

"Admirably," said Boa. "You're most kind."

Boa peered over the veranda rail, enchanted with the view.

"I had no idea that rivers looked just like us snakes from this
height," he said. "How very flattering."

"Why flattering?" asked Emma.

"Well, you know," said Boa, with a deep sigh, "we snakes are
not at all liked by you humans."

"Oh, I don't know . . ." Emma began to soothe him.

"No, no, it's quite true," said Boa, with a catch in his voice.
"Many humans call us slimy, but we're not. See for yourself!"

Emma stroked his skin delicately.

"No," she said, "your skin feels wonderfully smooth."

"There you are," said Boa. "It's rubbish. Then you say that
we're all poisonous. That's rubbish too. Only a few snakes are, and
they only use their venom in defense of themselves or their young."

The children remained silent. They knew this was true.

"Did you know," Boa went on, "that Indian tribes in the
Amazon keep constrictors as pest control officers and let us live in
their homes?"

"Pest control officers?" queried Conrad. "What do you mean?"

"They allow us to live in their huts, up in the beams," Boa
explained. "We catch all the rats and mice that eat their food stores."

"What a clever idea," said Ivan.

While they had been talking Belladonna had drifted down and finally settled on a sandbank on a curve in the river, where a whole new regiment of spiders was recruited from the shore and a new work force of electric eels was found in the shallow waters.

"Well, it's been a great pleasure meeting you," said Boa. "What are you going to do next?"

"I'm hoping we might come upon a jaguar or a tapir," said Lancelot.

"Well, if I see any about, I'll tell them to look out for you," said Boa. "Thanks once again for rescuing me. Good-bye."

They said good-bye to the friendly Boa and he wriggled his way across the sandbank and into the forest.

"He was nice," said Conrad, watching as the jungle swallowed up the giant snake. "I feel quite friendly toward snakes after that experience."

The children said good-bye to the orginal electric eel and spider crews and thanked them for their great help. Then they made sure the new spiders and eels were comfortably installed in their new homes.

The next morning, while they were having breakfast on the veranda, Ivan examined the forest through one of the telescopes. It was not long before he gave an excited cry.

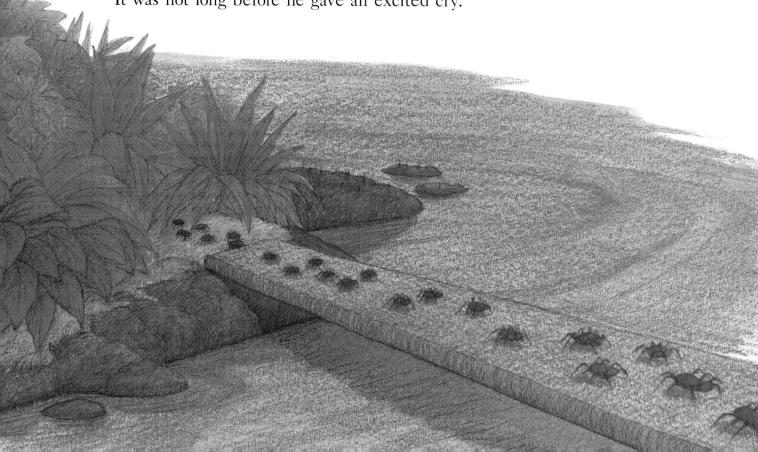

"Look, look, quickly!" he exclaimed. "It's a jaguar. There, crawling along a branch of that big tree. It's stalking something, I think."

The children rushed to the railing to look.

They watched the jaguar, glowing gold and black in the sunlight. He crawled slowly along the branch, his eyes fixed. The children followed his gaze and saw what he was stalking—a great, fat, brown tapir with a head like a horse and a short trunk rather like an elephant. It was peacefully pulling leaves into its mouth and chewing them, totally unaware of the danger that was crawling nearer and nearer, twenty feet above its head.

"I wish we could warn him," said Emma, anxiously.

"I shouldn't worry," Lancelot reassured her. "Tapirs have a special way of dealing with jaguars."

Holding their breath, they watched as the great cat launched itself onto the tapir's back. It dug its claws into the tapir's thick skin. The tapir uttered a grunt of surprise then set off through the forest like an express train.

Then they saw what Lancelot had meant. The tapir ran into all the prickliest bushes and the most tangled thickets it could find. The jaguar was pricked, scratched and banged on the head. But he still clung onto the tapir's back, snarling and growling whenever he was hurt.

Realizing this method would not dislodge his enemy, the tapir suddenly turned, burst out of the undergrowth and plunged into the river before the jaguar knew what was happening. They both disappeared under the water with a huge splash.

There was a great roar of approval from the treetops where a troop of red howler monkeys was obviously enjoying the spectacle.

The great cat's wet and bedraggled head showed above the surface of the river. He gasped and spluttered, spitting out water as he swam toward the shore. The howler monkeys cheered the tapir as the jaguar crawled up the bank and slouched off into the forest.

Lancelot called the howler monkeys over.

"I'm glad we found you so easily. We were told that my brother, Perceval, had come to visit you. Is he still here?"

"Maybe," replied Monkey slyly, "but I find it hard to remember when my stomach is empty."

"Will this help your memory?" asked Emma, producing a huge box of homemade fruit-and-nut biscuits.

The monkeys clustered around to have a taste of this new delicacy. So popular did the biscuits prove that several disgraceful fights broke out among the younger monkeys.

"I say, these are very good," said Monkey, his mouth full of biscuit. "What sort of tree do they grow on?"

"You make them," explained Emma, "out of flour."

"Out of flowers, eh?" said Monkey. "Who would have thought it? I would have thought flowers were only for smelling."

Emma gave up trying to explain biscuits to him.

"What about Perceval?" insisted Lancelot, impatiently.

"He came to see us and asked lots of questions," Monkey replied, stuffing another biscuit into his mouth. "But he left about a month ago."

"Where did he go?" Lancelot growled through clenched teeth.

"He went to study elephant seals in Patagonia. Now, are you going to the Cock of the Rocks Dance?" asked Monkey, cramming in a final biscuit as he turned to go.

"Well, no," said Emma. "We haven't been invited."

"You don't wait to be invited," said Monkey, airily. "You just go. They think they're the most beautiful birds in South America and love an audience. Follow me."

The howler monkeys, swinging by their tails, led the way, moving like acrobats through the trees while Lancelot and the children followed, stumbling in the thick rain forest. Eventually they came to some smooth slabs of rock surrounded by low bushes. It was an amazing sight. The bushes were full of birds like pigeons. The females were brown but the males were bright orange, with black wings and curved crests like Roman helmets.

As the children watched, they saw one male fly down from the bushes onto flat rocks. He began to dance. He flapped his wings, raised his crest and whirled around the stone ballroom.

The females watched the dance intently and discussed it.

"He's very good," said one hen, "but I must confess that I did prefer the one who did that amazing backward somersault."

"Yes," sighed another hen, "his plumage was a richer color, but I do think this one has a certain something."

The cock bird, having finished his dance, flew up into the bushes to let another take his place on the dance floor.

"I think I'll just go and have a word with him," said one of the hens. "He may dance well, but will he make a good father?"

She flew off to join the cock bird and started to question him vigorously about his caterpillar-hunting abilities.

"These special dancing areas are called lecks," explained Lancelot. "Here the males show off their plumage and strength. The female chooses the one who most impresses her. Then they go off, set up house, lay their eggs and rear their young."

"It's just like humans meeting at a disco," said Emma.

They stayed to watch until the dancing finished and then, having collected some fallen feathers, returned to Belladonna.

"Next stop, Patagonia," Lancelot cried, as they pulled in the anchors. He was impatient to get going now that he knew Perceval wasn't far ahead. The monkeys sang them a clamorous farewell which echoed loudly through the rain forest.

CHAPTER EIGHT
ABOUT TURN!

As Belladonna flew south over Argentina toward Patagonia, the great forest gave way first to marshy grassland. This was dotted with palms, rushes and trees with trunks shaped like bottles, whose branches were covered with yellow and pink flowers.

After a few days they reached the pampas. This was a great, flat plain of purple, green and brown grass. It stretched as far as the eye could see. Occasionally, there were great ombu trees, with short, very thick trunks and long shady branches. Once in a while they saw a tiny copse of giant thistles as high as a person on horseback. Presently Lancelot spotted a big lagoon on the coast and decided to stop.

On the banks of the lagoon they found a grassy hummock with a hole in it. Sitting outside this entrance, stiff as a sentry guarding a palace, was a small, speckly gray owl with huge yellow eyes.

Lancelot greeted the owl loudly. Owl clicked his beak reprovingly and glared with his brilliant yellow eyes.

"Do you mind not making so much noise," he said. "My wife's inside, sitting on our first clutch of eggs. Noise upsets her."

"I'm so sorry," said Emma, in hushed tones.

"Good," said Owl, "it doesn't do the eggs any good."

"What we want to ask you," said Lancelot in a loud whisper, "is who lives around here?"

"Well, let's see," said Owl. "Over there by the lagoon are ducks, ibis, spoonbills, a pair of foxes and some skunks."

"What about elephant seals?" asked Emma. "We need their help to find our lost great-uncle."

"They're a bit farther down the coast, but it's too far to walk from here. Tell you what though, the guanacos might give you a lift. They come here to drink and should be along soon."

"What are guanacos?" asked Ivan.

"They're relatives of llamas," explained Lancelot. "But llamas live up in the Andes Mountains while guanacos live down here on the pampas."

They didn't have long to wait before they saw a small group of gingerbread-colored guanacos approaching. They did look like llamas, but were longer-legged and slimmer. They came, walking very elegantly, to the edge of the lagoon and started to drink.

To the children's surprise, Owl did not fly over to them, but ran at great speed and had a whispered conversation with the biggest one. When he had finished drinking, this guanaco ambled over to the children and Lancelot.

"Hullo," he said in a soft voice. "I understand you want to meet some elephant seals."

"Yes please," begged Emma, "if you could manage it."

"Well," said Guanaco, surveying them all judiciously, "we can carry you children, but the fat one would be too heavy for us."

"Oh, that's all right," Lancelot said huffily, "I've already met elephant seals. I'll stay here and swim in the lagoon. You go on and enjoy yourselves."

"Will you be all right on your own?" asked Emma, feeling quite sorry for him. "You won't do anything dangerous, will you?"

"No, no, no," Lancelot assured her. "I shall be quite all right, thanks. You go off and have fun."

"Well, if you're sure," said Emma. "We won't be too long."

They mounted three of the guanacos and waved good-bye to Lancelot. They clung tightly to their steeds' soft wool as they galloped across the pampas, their ponchos streaming behind.

When they reached some huge, white sand dunes, the guanacos stopped. The children could hear the crash of the surf beyond.

"This is as far as we can take you," the biggest guanaco said. "We don't like walking on sand. But we'll wait and take you back when you're ready."

The children set off toward the sand dunes on foot.

"What are all those things running about on the dunes and tobogganing down them?" asked Ivan, as they drew closer.

"Why, they're penguins," exclaimed Emma, delightedly, adjusting her telescope. "Hundreds and hundreds of penguins."

They found that the huge sand dunes sheltered a flat area of the pampas from the sea. Here all the vegetation, except for a few thorny bushes, had been worn away and the earth was pitted with hundreds of holes. Outside each hole sat a pair of fat penguin chicks, fluffy balls of gray down.

In among all these babies ran adult birds, looking like waiters in black-and-white suits rushing about serving in a crowded restaurant, where every customer was wearing a fur coat.

On the sand dunes beyond, hundreds of other penguins tobogganed down toward the restaurant while others toiled up the slopes toward the sea. The babies were wheezing loudly and their parents were braying like donkeys, so the noise was indescribable.

"Excuse me," said Emma to a passing penguin, raising her voice to be heard above the uproar.

"No time," snapped the penguin as he thumped by on his flat feet. "Busy, busy, busy."

"Excuse me," said Conrad to another penguin.

"No time," said this penguin, waddling on. "Busy, busy, busy."

"Let's try talking to the babies," suggested Ivan. "At least they're standing still."

"Pardon me," he began, going up to some fat, fluffy chicks.

"No time. Hungry, hungry, hungry," wheezed the chicks.

"Isn't there anyone here we can talk to?" groaned Emma.

"What is it you want to know?" snapped a voice behind them.

Turning, they found a very old penguin with practically no feathers, sitting under a thornbush. Laid out in front of her was a small pile of shrimps.

"I'm the oldest member of the colony," she went on. "I know everything and everybody around here, so speak up."

"Why is everyone so busy?" asked Conrad.

"Well, you'd be busy if you had all these babies screaming for food," said Penguin. "We have to swim far out to sea to find fish, then swim all the way back. When we reach shore we have to walk over these wretched sand dunes, even though our feet are killing us. I'm glad I'm too old to lay eggs anymore."

"Wow," said Emma, sitting down beside her and taking out the diary. "How many of you are there?"

"Ten thousand," snapped Penguin, "give or take a hundred."

"Tell me, what do you drink?" asked Ivan. "I haven't seen any freshwater around here and it's terribly hot."

"Freshwater? Horrible stuff. We drink seawater," replied Penguin. "Now, if that's all, I really must eat my breakfast."

Penguin indicated the pile of shrimps with her flipper.

"I have to keep my strength up. I can't swim as fast as I did, you know. In my prime, I was one of the best fishers. I could swim at almost twenty miles an hour and jump twenty-three feet to escape a shark, but not nowadays.'' She shook her head sadly. "Oh, well, good-bye and remember, when you get to the shore don't forget to take a long drink of seawater. It's lovely.''

"Thank you very much," said Emma. "We'll remember.''

"Seawater! Ugh!" said Conrad, as they trudged over the dunes, penguins toboganing busily past them. "What an idea!"

They reached the top of the huge sand dunes to find a wide rocky shore with green sea breaking against it in long, languid rollers. They scrambled among the huge boulders, big waves splashing them with spray.

Suddenly, one of the rocks onto which Conrad had jumped gave a great gurgling roar, reared up some ten feet in height sending a shower of gravel over the children, and revealed itself to be a gigantic elephant seal. He was all folds and wrinkles of blubber. Between his watering eyes waved a huge nose, like a misshapen elephant's trunk.

"What is the meaning of this intrusion, this insolence, this unforgivable invasion of privacy?" roared Elephant Seal.

"We're so sorry," stammered Emma, gazing up at the huge animal which towered above her, "but we thought you were a rock.''

"A rock!" roared Elephant Seal, disbelievingly. "You thought *I*, the biggest, the most majestic seal along the coast of Patagonia, was a *rock?*"

"I've never heard so much boasting," said Ivan.

"I'm not boasting," said Elephant Seal, his nose whiffling and wobbling so much that Emma was afraid it might fall off. "I have to keep announcing how important I am, or else my rivals will want to fight me, or my wives will go off with another male."

The children did not know whether to laugh at or to run away from this huge, pompous creature. However, Emma remembered why they had come and stepped forward.

"We are looking for our Great-Uncle Perceval. We heard that he had come to visit you," she said.

"Naturally, Perceval came all the way around the world just to meet *me*," replied Elephant Seal. "Am I not the most magnifi . . ."

"Quite so," Conrad interrupted hurriedly, "but where is he?"

"Oh, he left some time ago. He returned to England I believe," replied Elephant Seal. "He wanted to tell his brother about me."

The children stared at him, stunned by this news.

"Now," he roared, rearing up his head and tail until he looked like a huge, gray, deformed banana, "this audience is at an end. Come wives, come children, follow me."

With much grunting and heaving he started on his way down to the sea and then, to the children's astonishment, all the rocks around them turned into elephant seals, mothers and babies of all sizes. They all lolloped their way down to the sea, splashed into the green waves and disappeared. The children were left standing alone on a deserted gravel beach.

They quickly made their way to where the patient guanacos were waiting for them and galloped back to tell Lancelot the news. Lancelot was lying in the lagoon, in a purple bathing suit. He reminded the children of a brightly colored elephant seal.

"Hurumph! Welcome back," he said, splashing onto the shore.

All talking at once, they told him what the elephant seal had said about Perceval.

"Gone home?" bellowed Lancelot, turning purple. "Well really! It's typical of Perceval to refuse to be rescued. This is the last straw."

With this, he stumped off indignantly to get dressed behind the thistles. A moment later there was a loud shout.

"WAAH! Stop!" Lancelot yelled. "Friend, you stupid animal. Stop it! Oh, phoo! Oh you wretched creature!"

The next moment he appeared around the thicket of giant thistles closely followed by a large skunk. Lancelot brushed past the children and plunged into the lagoon. As he passed, they smelled the most awful smell—a combination of rotting cabbage and onions with a touch of sewage for good measure.

"Does it belong to you?" Skunk asked, looking worried and gesturing toward Lancelot. "I am most awfully sorry, but it came rushing round the thistles and trod on my tail. I gave it a squirt from my scent gland in case it was an enemy. I do hope you'll forgive me. I realize now it's harmless."

Lancelot was plunging about in the water, shouting, "Ooh, the smell, the smell, I can't bear it."

Strong odors of skunk wafted to the children, who had to hold their handkerchiefs up to their noses.

"Phew! What an awful smell," complained Emma, her voice muffled by her handkerchief. "How long will he stink like that?"

"Oh, it's not permanent," Skunk assured her. "It's just a deterrent. He'll smell as good as new in four or five days."

"Four or five days!" said Conrad. "Gosh, how are we going to stand that? He'll stink out the whole of Belladonna!"

Emma fetched a clean bathing suit, a towel, a big bar of soap and a bottle of her eau de cologne. Lancelot disappeared into the reeds muttering furiously. He reappeared in a new bathing suit (green with black and pink polka dots!) but, though drenched in eau de cologne, he still reeked of skunk.

"I'm terribly sorry," Skunk apologized.

"It was an accident," Lancelot conceded, "and I did tread on your tail. I'm certainly going to remember you for a long time."

"I don't think we'll *ever* forget him," groaned Conrad.

"You'll have to live on the veranda," said Emma.

"Yes, we'll rig up a hammock for you to sleep in," added Ivan, "and make you take three cold baths a day."

"And feed you with a long pole," teased Conrad.

"I refuse to be treated like this," shouted Lancelot. "What do you think I am? A skunk?"

"Practically," laughed Emma.

"Now there's no call to be insulting," said Skunk, reproachfully. "Some people like my scent."

"Only people who can't smell," retorted Lancelot.

"Well you'll have to make the best of it," said Emma, "and leave that smelly bathing suit here. It stinks too much."

They said good-bye to Owl and the apologetic Skunk, and hustled Lancelot back to the veranda.

"Well kids," shouted Lancelot to the children who were standing as far away from him as they could, holding their noses, "we're going home."

"Oh, no. Can't we go on?" chorused the twins.

"We've been away for nearly a year and your mother will want to see you again," said Lancelot firmly. "Anyway, the rescue mission is over. We'll catch up with Perceval in England."

So, reluctantly they agreed, and set about preparing Belladonna for the journey home. They rigged up a comfortable hammock for Lancelot on the veranda. He still smelled too horrible to be allowed into the cabins except for a daily bath.

As compensation for this, Emma cooked all his favorite foods. He gorged himself on treacle and strawberry tart, roast turkey, apple pie, dumplings, chocolate pudding and other such comforting foods. When it was wet, he sat under a huge umbrella and when it was cold, he snuggled under a thick blanket.

Gradually, as they floated up the Atlantic on the trade winds, the skunk smell wore off. By the time Belladonna reached the shores of England they all agreed that Lancelot smelled normal.

The children became increasingly excited as the balloon neared their home. The twins spent hours looking for familiar landmarks through the telescopes. Emma worked furiously on the diary, sketching, painting and writing up the rest of their adventures.

At last their cottage came into sight. It was exactly three hundred and sixty-five days since they had set out. Conrad, looking through the telescope, gave a great shout.

"What on earth is that . . . thing . . . on the lawn?" he cried.

Lancelot rushed to look at the strange contraption and gave a great whoop of joy.

"Why, that's Perceval's flying machine," he cheered. "Wait here, I've got something I've been saving."

He ran below and reappeared carrying an enormous rocket.

"There was just one left after our adventure with the wolves," he explained, lighting the fuse.

The rocket shot up into the sky and exploded with an enormous bang, showering the countryside with multicolored stars. The children watched as Mrs. Dollybutt ran out onto the lawn, followed by a tall, thin figure dressed in a flying suit. They both waved.

Belladonna's great shadow fell across the lawn once again. Down went the anchors, followed by the ladders and then Lancelot and the children. Mrs. Dollybutt hugged and kissed them all, crying and laughing with delight at their safe return.

"Well, Perceval," Lancelot greeted the tall figure gruffly, "we've found you at last. A merry song and dance you've led us."

"We came to rescue you . . . Lancelot said you must be lost . . . You disappeared for two years," clamored the children, greatly excited at being home at last, seeing their mother and finally meeting Perceval.

"Disappeared? Lost? What are you talking about?" asked Perceval in a puzzled voice. "You really are the limit, Lancelot. I sent you dozens of letters telling you what I was doing."

"Well, you know I never open mail in case it's bills or bad news," replied Lancelot.

"Lancelot, you're impossible," snorted Perceval, sounding so much like his brother that everyone burst into laughter.

"Oh well, no harm done," said Lancelot, winking broadly at the children. "I don't think our trip was a waste of time, do you?"

"Oh no, it was simply splendid," Conrad assured him.

"Absolutely great," agreed Ivan.

"It was the most fantastic thing ever," said Emma, kissing Lancelot on both cheeks. "Thank you a million times."

They carried the huge globe of the world from Belladonna into the cottage so that over the sumptuous tea Mrs. Dollybutt prepared for them they could show her exactly where they had been and what they had seen. They displayed all their souvenirs and showed her the diary.

"We did miss out on quite a lot, of course," murmured Lancelot

thoughtfully, spinning the globe. "India, for example. That's because we tried to do too much, I think. Now, next time . . ."

"Next time?" chorused the children. "Is there going to be a next time?"

"Of course," said Lancelot, "but next time I think we'll just go to one country and explore it properly. What do you think?"

"Wonderful," they shouted together.

When the tea things had been cleared away, they gathered around the fire with the globe of the world and started making plans.

Just before bedtime, Emma took Lancelot out into the garden
and linked her arm in his.

"You invented Perceval's disappearance just so we could go on
our fantastic flying journey, didn't you?" she whispered, as she
hugged him. "You're a dreadful old man."

"Am I?" asked Lancelot innocently, but his eyes seemed to be
twinkling as brightly as the stars above them.

GERALD DURRELL

is a world-renowned naturalist and conservationist who created his
own zoological park on the island of Jersey in the English
Channel. The park specializes in the captive breeding of
endangered mammals, birds and reptiles. He is the best-selling
author of almost 30 books, including *My Family and Other Animals*,
A Zoo in my Luggage and *The Amateur Naturalist*.

GRAHAM PERCY

was born and grew up in New Zealand. He studied graphic art
at the Royal College of Art in England, and has lived and worked
in London since graduating. He is the illustrator of many books
for children.